THE TAIPAN CLUB

Also by John Henderson

A Blind Eye

Anchor Man

Musgrave Solution

Murder Scams & Gravy Trains

THE TAIPAN CLUB

Simon Webster's fifth fiasco

JOHN HENDERSON

The Taipan Club

eBook ISBN: 978-0-9875769-6-5

Book ISBN: 978-0-9875769-7-2

Publisher: J. Henderson, Canberra, Australia

The Taipan Club
SIMON WEBSTER'S FIFTH FIASCO

A botched kidnapping and the murder of a recalcitrant politician sets DCI Simon Webster and DS Noel Elliott off, reluctantly, on an investigation they would prefer not to be investigating. Initially, what appears to be a simple case of murder is soon consumed into an international attempt to acquire Graham Lee's Taipan Club. To be successful, this venture needs political support and the support of a property developer which, together, comprise the bane of Simon's life. Antagonism and murder abounds as feminine malice and financial greed present the two detectives with what could be a career ending investigation.

Chapter 1

It was plainly obvious that Benny, who was big, really big, tall and muscular with broad shoulders, supplied the required intimidation behind the duo's villainous activities. If Benny provided the muscle power, it fell to Alfred, or more appropriately Alf, to supply the brain power. But then again, all things are relative and Alf was probably as bright as the black hole at the centre of the galaxy. Although Benny was a personable and quite a nice bloke who would go out of his way to avoid treading on an ant, he was not, by any stretch of the imagination, a person having ever considered being a candidate for Mensa membership. Benny's academic achievements had been rather dismal while, at times, he appeared to lack the intuitive spontaneous reactive response normally driven by common sense. It was unfortunate that any degree of mental dexterity or practicality was regarded by the bureaucratic functionaries, who obviously believed they held the monopoly on these two attributes, to be a rarity, if not non-existent, within the plebeian society of which the wealthy middle class probably considered both Alf and Benny members.

Alf was therefore the brains of the gang of two if for no

other reason that he probably exhibited an intelligence quotient marginally superior to Benny's. The two had become petty criminals around Sydney town by conducting heists from hotel bottle shops, self-serve petrol stations, or the theft from some poor unsuspecting convenience store cashier. While Benny had no great aspirations in advancing his criminal status, Alf recognised the fact that they were no more than humble minor players within the hierarchical world of the master criminal. Although coveting far greater prestige and stature within his chosen profession, Alf was fully aware that he was currently standing on a rung of the criminal ladder currently occupied by none other than rogues, scoundrels and reprobates who harboured no greater criminal aspiration than knocking off the milk money left outside the door. But Alf had come to the realisation that if you were going to get done for stealing a lamb, you may as well get done for stealing a sheep. Following that piece of profound and penetrating logic, Alf decided it was time for a step up the gangland ladder from the irrelevant, insignificant wrongdoer to that of the villainous, cold and calculating criminal. Needless to say, such a step necessitated an appropriate increase in the gravity of crime committed, a fact not lost on Alf.

Whether Alf would have reached such a momentous decision on his own accord was entirely problematic. Irrespective of whether he would or wouldn't have, his decision was somewhat circumvented as the wheels had already been firmly set in motion by a phone call from a security guard at one of Sydney's illegal gambling casinos, the Taipan Club. In reality, the security guard happened to be a bloke named Jacko who had been employed as a doorman cum bouncer by the late gangster, Paul Stack, owner and operator of another illegal gambling den, The Spinning Wheel. The term "late gangster" should not be construed in any way to suggest Paul Stack had reformed his evil ways and was no longer a gangster.

In truth, Paul Stack had lost interest in all matters of a

nefarious nature. Come to think of it, Paul Stack had lost interest in a lot of things having been shuffled of this mortal coil by imbibing in an overdose of ricin, in spite of the fact an underdose of the stuff would have achieved the same result. Jacko, overcome with grief following Stack's demise, was fortunate to be offered a job working on a temporary basis for a Mr Graham Lee at the Taipan Club, another illegal but very posh upmarket casino. The temporary nature of the job was dependent on the sale of the club to a property developer following an arrangement, financially beneficial to both parties, made between Mr Lee and the developer. Naturally, having decided on the future of the club, Mr Lee was anxious for the matter to be handled expeditiously and have the developer commence on the bricks and mortar side of the deal. Irrespective of how expeditiously Mr Lee may have hoped his undertaking would be acted upon by the bureaucracy, the delays being incurred could be mathematically calculated by the extent of complicated and inflexible meddling, from local council to state government level; and there was substantial meddling.

The object of Jacko's phone call was to acquaint Alf of the fact that he had been approached by a regular, and very wealthy, female client of the Taipan Club who, apparently, was in some sort of undisclosed predicament. From Jacko's appraisal of the situation, it seemed the very wealthy lady, in order to extricate herself from her predicament, was looking for someone of integrity and probity for assistance. Although the nature of the task at hand had not been disclosed, it was stressed that whoever Jacko might nominate to assist the very wealthy lady, the nominated person would require a degree of tact and discretion while curbing the desire to ask inquisitive questions. On successful completion of the task, and if the client was happy with the outcome, a lucrative remuneration would be forthcoming.

The bit of news Jacko refrained from conveying to Alf was

that the lady had made it quite clear that the nominated collaborator need not necessarily be an intellectual giant and, in fact, would prefer whoever Jacko might propose to be somewhere at the other end of the phrenic scale. Once the very rich lady had confirmed that the essential elements of the selection criteria had been clearly understood by Jacko, it was easy; Jacko had rung Alf. Although it was obvious Jacko was unable to provide Alf any specific details of whatever assistance the wealthy lady required, Alf was intrigued and gave Jacko permission to convey his telephone number to the very wealthy lady.

WITHOUT HARBOURING ANY GREAT EXPECTATION, Alf and Benny now sat outside a Spit Junction coffee shop sipping hot chocolate while on the lookout for a woman wearing a black dress, a handbag on one arm and a rolled-up newspaper under the other.

'Do you think she'll turn up?' queried Benny before he spooned the soggy marshmallow into his mouth.

Alf gave a shrug. 'Who knows? She didn't give any indication as to what type of assistance she needs so your guess is as good as mine. Want my marshmallow?'

'Yeah, thanks,' Benny replied and scooped the lolly from Alf's chocolate. 'Hang on, I think this might be her.'

The tall brunette dressed in a black dress, holding her handbag in one hand and a rolled-up newspaper in the other, stood beside the table and cast an appraising eye over the two seated gentlemen who politely remained seated. 'Alfred and Benny?'

'Yeah, that's us. Pull up a chair,' Alf responded with all the charm and manners of a demented warthog. 'We believe you have a need of some assistance, Mrs... sorry, but we don't know your name.'

'No, but you may refer to me as Mrs Stone,' Mrs Stone said as she purloined a chair from an unoccupied table and sat. 'Yes, I'll have an Irish coffee, please,' she said to an attentive young waitress.

'Now, just how may we be of assistance, Mrs Stone?' Alf enquired.

'Before I go into that, it's probably a good idea if I explain the situation,' Mrs Stone said as she settled herself more comfortably onto her chair. 'My husband is a politician, state, that is. Whether he's state or federal is of no consequence as they're all tarred with the same brush anyway.'

Before Mrs Stone could continue with her explanation of the situation, Alf interrupted. 'As you have referred to your husband as a "he", I assume that makes him of the male gender, so I won't ask. Come to think of it, I don't think I've ever met a politician of any of the other genders. But you say they're all painted with the same brush, Mrs Stone. For the benefit of both Benny and myself, could you please explain?' Alf asked a little self-consciously.

Well, at least Jacko got that right; these two must have just arrived on planet Earth, Mrs Stone thought to herself. 'Although it's said there are exceptions to the rule, I think it safe to say my husband is representative of most, if not all, politicians. In short, he's an egocentric maniac and a complete degenerate who thinks I'm totally ignorant as to what he gets up to.'

Alf's face contorted in surprise. 'Gee, and I s'pose they're his good points. And you mean to say it's these maniacs and degenerates we vote in to govern us?'

Mrs Stone shrugged her shoulders. 'Yes, pity isn't it. They probably aren't born that way, it's just once they get elected to parliament the power goes to their head. I suppose you could say they undergo some sort of metamorphosis and become quite obnoxious really. But we diverge from the issue. As you might have already gathered, my marriage may not necessarily reflect that of the happily married couple as politicians, including my husband, would have people believe. On the other hand, Morton, my husband, depends on being seen to live in a happy domestic environment with a devoted and loving wife. You've seen it yourself, politicians dragging their smiling wife out to places where the politician believes it's appropriate to drag the smiling better half, especially at election time, irrespective of the true nature of the relationship, which is more than likely on the rocks. As long as they appear to be happily married and he's seen as a regular Mister Nice Guy, people, mostly women, will vote for them irrespective of the political barrow they're pushing.'

Benny, trying to dig the last bit of chocolate from the bottom of his glass, paused and looked up. 'So, you want us to do something to your husband that might put him offside with the voters?' he said before putting the spoon into his mouth upside down to savour the remaining chocolate.

'Sort of. As you may or may not know, there's an election due within the next twelve months and, as hubby is hoping to be re-elected, it presents an opportune time to start divorce proceedings and try to make life as difficult as I can for the little worm. Now, as it happens, a few of my girlfriends and I usually go out on a Friday night, mostly to the Taipan Club, that casino in the city run by Graham Lee and his wife Louisa. I've known Louisa for years. She was married to a politician, a Mr Porter, who was murdered...'

'No way,' Alf protested. 'Benny and I might do a lot of things some people might consider illegal but murder ain't one of 'em. No, sorry but you'll have to find a couple of others to do the job.'

'Bloody hell. I don't want you to go off and murder the little sleaze, so just shut up and let me finish. Now, this Louisa Porter, who is now Louisa Lee, was married to a politician herself and can understand my situation. Although she didn't murder her husband, she really appreciates the fact that someone did. Anyway, Louisa came up with the idea I might be able to screw my husband financially before divorcing him by having myself kidnapped and then have a sizeable ransom demanded from the little worm. With him already out on the hustings trying to bump up voter support within the electorate, he would have to be seen as doing everything possible to secure my safe return once it becomes public knowledge that I've been kidnapped.' After her rather lengthy explanation of her so-called dilemma, Mrs Stone sat back with an air of satisfaction and sipped her coffee leaving a tell-tale smudge of cream on her upper lip.'

'So, you want us to kidnap you and demand a ransom from your husband? As he's trying to make himself appear to be a squeaky-clean pillar of virtue, a contradiction in terms if ever I've heard one, you believe he'll pay whatever you ask, or should I say, demand. The witless plebs out in the electorate will obviously think he's a Mister Nice Guy doing everything possible to recover his dearly beloved from the clutches of the wicked kidnappers. And with his misses being kidnapped by some dastardly evil criminals, hubby might be seen as Sir Galahad and pick up some sympathy support, at least from the ladies of the electorate,' Alf replied after a surprisingly unerring appraisal of the situation.

Mrs Stone nodded before clicking her fingers to the now inattentive waitress and gesticulating for another Irish coffee. 'Yes, that's the plan although I don't care two hoots about any popularity considerations, the important thing is my kidnapping. I've worked out that I would need to be kidnapped from a location where we'll be recorded on CCTV. That will prove I've been abducted. I live over at Mosman and, judging from your phone number, you live somewhere north of the bridge?'

'Yeah, Alf lives in a house over at Crows Nest, in Chandos Street. I live up at St. Leonards.' Benny interjected in an effort to add to the discussion.

'That's handy. If you can abduct me from somewhere in

Mosman that would mean I could drive to the shops and leave my car there. Obviously, I would have to lay low until the ransom is paid and that would mean living with Alf at Chandos Street until the worm comes up with the cash,' Mrs Stone said in a display of animated excitement.

'Whoa. Just stop right there,' demanded Alf. 'We haven't decided to kidnap anybody yet, and if we do decide to, any thought of you living with me just ain't on the cards, so forget it.'

Mrs Stone, obviously deflated on hearing Alf's rejection of her rather exciting plan, pushed her bottom lip forward in an attempt to adopt a rather sulky expression. 'Look Alf, first off I wouldn't be living with you; I'd just be residing in the same house. Secondly, it would only be until the ransom is paid and that's when you'll get your cut of twenty percent of the taking. That means if we ask for a hundred you'd get twenty to share, ten each. That's a lot of marshmallow.'

Alf looked at Benny and raised his eyes questioningly. Benny looked at Alf, pursed his lips and gave a shrug. 'Seems good to me,' Benny said. 'You do have a spare room out the back and it wouldn't be for too long anyway.'

It was of little consequence how many episodes of Dragnet or Agatha Christie murder mysteries Alf had meticulously studied, the thought of carrying out a major crime, such as a kidnapping, did appeal to Alf's master criminal alter ego. The intricate complexities of masterminding such an audacious crime would present Alf and Benny the one giant leap up the ladder, not necessarily for mankind but a leap into the realms of the real master criminal, maybe.

'Okay, Mrs Stone,' Alf said with a nod of the head, 'we agree to kidnap you and send off a ransom note to your husband. The specifics of the ransom we can work out after we've abducted you. The nuts and bolts of the abduction we'll leave up to you as you'll know where you want to be abducted from and where you'll park your car. All we'll need to know are the details of the car you drive and the general area you'll park it. It's in that vicinity we'll nab you. Of course, you realise we'll have to make it look realistic.'

'Yes, but be gentle with me. I have a low pain threshold.'

Chapter 2

To be fair, it could be said the abduction of Mrs Stone went off without too many hiccups. Having decided on the location and time for the seizure of the victim, the first glitch in their plans was encountered about ten minutes into the operation when it was determined the car being driven by Alf did not have room enough for the driver and two passengers. A lovely sports car that the Triumph TR4 is, its carrying capacity in this particular instance failed to meet that required for the specific task in mind.

After returning to Crows Nest to change Alf's you beaut sporty machine for Benny's 1998 Holden Commodore, and sully the number plate to make it at least a bit difficult to read, the drive to the shopping centre at Mosman had Benny a little confused. The shopping centre itself was located on a street named Avenue Road which, to Benny, was a tad misleading as he was of the firm belief it should be located on either an avenue or a road; one or the other, but not both. Although a little unfamiliar with the back streets of Mosman, Benny was not in total ignorance of the area as he had once travelled down Military Road, Mosman's main thoroughfare, when he had decided to spend a day at the famous Taronga Zoo.

Despite these little setbacks, the actual abduction of Mrs Stone went off pretty well. Having located and completed a few laps of the shopping centre underground parking lot in search of the quarry, Mrs Stone was eventually located standing next to her black BMW, arms akimbo and a surly look about her; her kidnappers were late.

Both Benny and Alf quickly leapt from the stationary Commodore and grabbed Mrs Stone who, it could be said, put up a convincing struggle to break free. After several attempts to place a bag over the poor unsuspecting subject's head, Mrs Stone finally took the bag from Benny and dragged it over her head herself. Within the space of a few seconds the abduction was complete with Mrs Stone secured in the back seat of the car along with a small travel bag she had been holding. That she could have dragged the bag off her head and open the unlocked car door to escape at any time while in the car park, where a speed limit of ten kilometres an hour applied, apparently never occurred to the shocked and disorientated kidnapped victim. But the kidnappers did look threatening and the aim of the exercise had been successfully achieved.

IT WAS two days after the abduction of Mrs Stone that the abductee decided sufficient time had elapsed for the charade to come to an end and her true identity revealed. This decision was prompted by the fact that any ransom note would have to be penned by the abductors and sent to the husband of the abductee.

'Okay, boys, let's get down to the financial side of things and get the ransom note in the mail,' Mrs Stone said as she joined Benny and Alf sitting at the kitchen table drinking coffee.

'And about time too,' replied Alf, eager for a cut of the ransom and be rid of this pesky woman.

'Now, don't be like that, Alf,' Mrs Stone remonstrated. 'Before we get down to business, I think you should know my name isn't Mrs Stone. I'm really married to Morton Blakey, who really is a politician and we live in Mosman. And my name is Rosetta Blakey, not Stone. Stone was my name from a previous marriage.'

'So, that would make you Rosetta Stone, if your name was still Stone,' Alf snickered.

'Very funny, but let's get on with this demand for money. Now, Alf, you take a photo of me holding today's newspaper and run a copy of it off on your computer. We'll send it with the letter as it will prove I'm still alive,' Rosetta said. 'I'm just a bit disappointed the newspapers or TV haven't reported me missing yet. I would have thought Morton would have been worried by now, although I suppose he is a busy man with the election coming up.'

'No, no need to worry. I'm sure he misses you and will pay up as quickly as possible,' reassured Benny. 'Anyway, how much ransom are you going to ask for?'

'Oh, I think an even hundred should do it,' Rosetta replied with a smile. 'You think I'm worth that much, Alf?'

'Cripes, at least. I would have said five, but it's your kidnapping. Just give us your husband's address and I'll get this letter finished and Benny can drop it into the snail-mail at the post office.'

———

'DO you think he's received the letter by now?' Benny asked.

'Yeah, I should think so but you can never tell these days. The postie hasn't much to deliver as everyone uses computers and e-mail,' Alf replied.

'That would probably explain why the people at the post

office didn't seem to know what to do with it. They couldn't decide whether to put a stamp on it or send it to a museum. They said it was the first piece of snail-mail they'd seen in years,' Benny chortled.

Rosetta sat back on the kitchen chair and folded her arms. 'And what are you going to do with all that money, Benny?'

'What, you mean my cut of the twenty? Well, as I have trouble boiling water, I think I might go out and have a good meal as I'm not much of a gourmet cook, or any kind of cook for that matter.'

'Struth, you'll be able to buy yourself a few good meals with that amount,' Rosetta returned with a smile. 'And what about you, Alf?'

'Well, I was going to put my ten towards a car servicing,' interjected Alf, 'not that ten will get me much of a service.'

'What do you mean "ten won't get you much",' Rosetta chided before she was suddenly overtaken by a pall of stunned horror. 'Alf, when I said a hundred, just what amount did you write down in the letter?'

Unable to fathom the cause of Rosetta's sudden change of demeanour, Alf, in all innocence and with eyes wide open, replied. 'Just as you told me, I wrote down a hundred dollars.'

Rosetta opened her mouth to say something but obviously thought better of it. She sat there at the table dumbstruck; mouth open, her unblinking eyes staring into oblivion as an appalling feeling of total stupidity flooded over her like a giant tsunami.

Benny, being a nice, caring bloke, became concerned. 'Are you all right, Rosetta? Can I get you a drink of water, or something else?'

Whatever the problem, and obviously there was something dreadfully wrong as both Benny and Alf could now see Rosetta slowly shaking her head and muttering quietly to herself over and over, 'One hundred bloody dollars. Jacko, you're dead.'

It took Rosetta some time to even start her recovery from whatever it was that prompted the severe case of apoplexy she had obviously suffered. While neither Alf nor Benny had any inkling as to what had caused Rosetta such anguish, both men considered a bit of prudence might be appropriate, at least until Rosetta had totally recovered.

It was following a good few drams of medicinal Johnny Walker before Rosetta, now sufficiently composed, turned to Alf for some details of the ransom letter drafted by Alf and assisted with Benny's and her own input. 'So, when I said we needed a hundred for my safe return, you put down one hundred dollars?' she asked, knowing full well the answer.

Alf's eyes opened wide furrowing his forehead as he pursed his lips. 'Yes, of course. That's what you said and, as it sounded reasonable, I wrote down exactly what you told me to write down; one hundred. Okay, you didn't say dollars but you wouldn't be asking for one hundred doughnuts so I put in dollars.'

'And the thought of putting in the word thousand never occurred to you?'

'You mean a hundred thousand doughnuts?'

'A hundred thousand dollars, you, you dopey dullard.'

A pall of silence engulfed the kitchen as a morbid atmosphere, akin to that which might be expected around midnight in some ancient burial ground, descended over the room. Suddenly, to both Alf and Benny, the reason for Rosetta's disquiet became obvious. For Alf, the realisation that to progress to the realm of the master criminal, as per his ambition, a radical adjustment to his thinking strategy was needed. Next time, if there was ever to be a next time, Alf had to think big.

Knowing there was little they could do or say to Rosetta in order to appease the situation, both Benny and Alf kept their mouth shut leaving it to Rosetta to break the silence. 'And just how is Mr Blakey supposed to send us the one hundred dollars, if the weasel can afford that much?' she asked sarcastically. Rosetta posed the question without showing too much interest as she had now come to expect some diabolically stupid answer from her two villainous associates.

Alf's sheepish countenance rapidly transformed to one of deep concentration. After some thought he said, 'Come to think of it, I don't think I gave any instructions on that score. Maybe you could phone him and tell him where to send it.'

'Hey, hang on. You're the kidnappers so if he's going to pay my ransom, it's you who he'll be paying, not me,' Rosetta said scornfully.

'Oh yeah, I s'pose he will,' Alf conceded. 'Benny, have you any ideas?'

Benny's face broke into a broad grin. 'No problems there. Before I posted the letter, I wrote the return address on the back of the envelope so he'll know where to send the money.'

Never quite understanding the technology behind Newton's Laws of Motion, Alf's high school physics teacher had eventually been able to imbue into the brain of his academic prodigy that for every action there is an equal and opposite reaction. As this thought now flashed across his mind, Alf couldn't supress the feeling that Benny's initiative in providing a return address on the envelope might provoke a certain reaction, if not from the constabulary, at least from Mr Blakey. Alf's summation of the now very mediocre situation was confirmed as he looked at Rosetta who sat quietly, a deadpan look on her face while slowly shaking her head.

After a few moments of deep contemplation, Rosetta rose from her chair and slowly walked from the room while extracting her mobile phone from her jacket. A short time later she returned to the kitchen and quietly regained her seat. 'Well gentlemen, the whole idea of getting myself kidnapped was to scrounge some money out of my husband. Irrespective of whether it's a hundred thousand dollars or a hundred dollars, I have absolutely no intention of returning to the little weasel.

'As he's a politician, the last thing he would want bandied around is a domestic scandal, especially if there's another woman involved, although in his case it's probably women. That's why I thought it was an appropriate time to fleece the sod and shake up his re-election chances. Despite our minor hiccup with the ransom, I appreciate and thank you for the help you have provided. Notwithstanding, and in view of the possible recriminations, I really think the time has come for us to part company.' Without another word, Rosetta rose from her seat, picked up her packed bag from the hallway and departed Alf's Chandos Street residence.

Chapter 3

Detective Chief Inspector Simon Webster replaced the receiver, clasped his hands in his lap, arched his thumbs together and slowly swivelled his chair from side to side, a faraway look on his face. His colleague at the other end of the office, Detective Sergeant Noel Elliott, sensitive to the fact that DCI Webster was not overjoyed with the recently terminated phone conversation, gazed expectantly at his boss. As if woken from a hypnotic trance, Simon suddenly pushed his chair back from the desk and jumped to his feet. 'Come on, Noel, that was Fisher; he wants us up in Paxton's office. As if our accounting for five murders in one investigation isn't enough, he's probably found another diabolical crime for us to solve. Whoever said success has its own rewards obviously wasn't successful.'

Simon Webster was tall and athletic. His once long blond hair, attributable to the endless hours spent in the surf or lounging on the beach, now suffered from the ravages of time and had already made considerable progress on its inexorable recession to a preordained genetic fate; baldness. Irrespective as to the cause of the rather sordid ultimate future of his remaining golden locks, it would have been rather surprising if Simon's leisure time had been spent any other way living, as he and his lovely wife Georgie did, in the seaside suburb of Collaroy where Simon was a member of the Surf Life Saving Club.

Noel Elliott was the physical antithesis of Simon. Built like what is euphemistically referred to as a brick outhouse, Noel was short with shoulders any gym junkie would happily overdose on steroids to emulate. With black hair, his career playing in the front row for the mighty Manly Marlins rugby union team had endowed Noel with a face only a mother, or his charming wife, Sue, could love. Regrettably, his once dignified aquiline nose had been permanently reduced to a flattened, scarred, schnozzle due to an incurable flaw in his tackling technique.

The two detectives worked well together and, along with their respective ladies, had established a close social relationship, the two couples regularly sharing the occasional glass of wine or a beer on the back lawn of Simon's bungalow. Fortunately, Noel and Sue lived only a few kilometres further along on the northern beaches peninsula at Mona Vale, just a couple of minutes drive from Collaroy.

Employed at the Day Street police station located in the fair city of Sydney, it was Simon who knocked on the chief superintendent's door which was promptly opened by Superintendent Nigel Fisher. While Simon and Noel were both dressed in mufti, the superintendent looked resplendent in his blue police dress uniform adorned with the requisite silver braiding commensurate with his rank, as was Chief Superintendent Paxton. Crikey, something's rotten in the state of Denmark, Simon thought, his recollection of the Hamlet quote correct for once. There was a third person already sitting in front of Paxton's desk, the troubled face not recognisable but not totally unfamiliar to Simon.

'Before we get started,' Paxton said as he stood to make

introductions, 'I'd like you to meet The Honourable Morton Blakey, MP. It seems Mr Blakey has a bit of a problem.'

Aah yes, that's where I've seen this bloke. He's a politician, or something or other, and has had his picture in the papers lately. That's right, he's a member of parliament, a member of the government, I think, Simon mused as Blakey rose and greeted the detectives with a smile and a shake of the hands. And that's an oxymoron, an honourable MP, Simon decided.

After the cordial introductions had been completed and everyone comfortably seated, Chief Superintendent Paxton opened proceedings. 'Right, as we are totally in the dark as to whatever the circumstances are that necessitate you favouring us with your exalted presence, I think it might be appropriate if your honour might explain the situation.'

Noel frowned, shook his head and couldn't refrain from butting in. 'Excuse me if I'm wrong, sir, and I apologise in advance if I am, but from an article I read in the paper today, Mr Blakey is a backbencher in the Lower House. Now, while all members of the Upper House are granted the honorific, honourable, such provision does not extend to all members of the Lower House. Although Mr Blakey sits on various committees, he doesn't hold any ministerial portfolio and, as far as I know, is not entitled to be referred to as the honourable, that provision within the Lower House being limited to ministers and the speaker. As a consequence, do we refer to Mr Blakey as The Honourable Mr Blakey, or just Mister Blakey?'

Simon closed his eyes and wished he hadn't heard what he did as he was fully aware Noel was about to be the subject of a chief superintendent's vitriolic castigation. Despite the presence of a member of parliament, Simon was under no illusion that whatever forthcoming admonishment Noel might expect, the nature of the censure would probably rot the paint off the walls. The chief superintendent, thrown somewhat off balance by

Noel's probing question, sat in mute silence, wondering. There has to be a serious flaw with police training procedures for a simple interview with a politician to go so terribly wrong, and all this brought about by a seriously misguided detective sergeant. Fortunately, it was Blakey who held up his hand in the universal "stop" signal, providing Paxton time to recover his totally addled wits induced by a detective sergeant's fascinating question.

'No, that's all right, chief superintendent. It's refreshing to find someone out in the electorate who is aware of some of the protocols and procedures of a parliament that works for the people. In response to your question, Sergeant Elliott, you are perfectly correct. I am a Mister and it is only through my desire not to embarrass the chief superintendent that I didn't raise the issue earlier, not that it is an issue. I know I've been referred to as the honourable in the press, but I have an inkling my wife, Rosetta, may have been responsible for some cynical comments made to reporters on those occasions.'

'Oh yes, and why is that Mr Blakey?' queried the chief superintendent, now anxious to determine why he had been led to believe The Honourable was really no more than a Mister.

Mr Blakey scratched the back of his head and pursed his lips. 'I think we may be straying from the purpose of my visit, Chief Paxton, but as you obviously think it important, I'll tell you. Rosetta is a very beautiful woman and has proved very helpful in my political career. Unfortunately, over the years she has developed a somewhat critical view of politicians and believes she is now, at best, a necessary accessory and no more than an essential embellishment to my wardrobe. We married about ten years ago when we were both in our early thirties and I was a lowly backbencher. It's rather surprising Rosetta hasn't referred to me as the president or the Premier as she usually has a disparaging or condescending comment to make about me to any snotty-nose, witless reporter eager to listen to any trivial garbage they might hear. Anyway, gentlemen, I'm sure you have more important things on your mind than to contemplate my domestic circumstances.' Morton Blakey rose from his chair, extended his hand to Chief Paxton and headed for the door.

Chief Superintendent Paxton, still in the dark as to why Mr Blakey had deemed it necessary to favour an audience with a detective chief superintendent, a detective superintendent, a detective chief inspector and a detective sergeant, cast an askance look to his subordinate, Nigel Fisher, who returned a "stuffed if I know" look to his boss. After a discrete exchange of glances, both Simon and Noel were agreed that they, too, were no more enlightened than Superintendent Fisher or Chief Superintendent Paxton.

'Well, sir,' Simon said, addressing his superior officer, Superintendent Fisher, 'that was all very enlightening. While it seems Mr Blakey doesn't get on too well with his charming wife, Rosetta, I fail to see just how or why their domestic situation should involve us. While not wishing to cast aspersions on your ability to manage personal problems, sir, I would have thought Mr Blakey might have gone to a marriage councillor, not a detective chief superintendent.'

'Yes, well I'm sure we're all still in the dark just as much as you are, chief inspector,' Fisher replied. 'You haven't any idea, sir?' the question addressed to Paxton.

'Beats me, but you have to remember, we're dealing with a politician and most of 'em suffer from mental atrophy. All I can do is apologise for dragging you all up here and suggest you carry on as normal.' It was just as Paxton's remaining visitors were about to leave there came a tentative knock to the door which, after a nod from Paxton, Noel opened to reveal a sheepish looking Morton Blakey.

'I'm sorry to be an inconvenience, Chief Superintendent Paxton, but I completely forgot what it was I came to see you about. Do you mind?' he appealed, indicating to the chair he had vacated just a few moments earlier.

'No, not at all. We were just wondering what exactly the purpose of your visit was,' Paxton confessed.

Blakey sat, head down in embarrassment. After a moment he apparently came to a decision. 'Yes, I must apologise but I have a few things on my mind, what with the election coming up. I have to admit, it completely slipped my mind.'

Paxton, becoming a little irritated with Blakey's inability to get to the crux of the mater, even allowing for the fact he was a politician, made the decision for Blakey. 'And just what is it, Mr Blakey, that's so significant to drag you down from Macquarie Street yet of so little consequence the matter totally slipped your mind?'

'Well, it's nothing I can't handle I s'pose, but it seems my wife, Rosetta, has been kidnapped.'

Chapter 4

Noel leant back on his swivel chair and gently massaged the back of his neck with his left hand. 'Well, that's a turn up for the books. Here we have a bloke complain to the chief superintendent that his wife's been kidnapped but doesn't want us to do anything about it.'

At the other end of the office, Chief Inspector Simon Webster shrugged his shoulders, slowly shook his head and looked totally bored. 'Yeah, but I s'pose he has to look like he's trying to do something to recover his wife. It wouldn't go over too well in his electorate if he chose not to do anything at all.'

'Okay, so it's all right for him to report the kidnapping just as long as we don't investigate the matter,' Noel replied with a hint of sourness. 'But as it's over the other side of the harbour and not in our bailiwick, we wouldn't be involved in any investigation anyway, so who cares?'

Simon shrugged. 'Yeah, I can't help thinking there's a conspiracy somewhere involved. Blakey must have his reasons for the non-intervention by police, and you can bet those reasons would reflect badly on him, not his wife. That's why he's reluctant to let anyone know just what's going on. I wouldn't mind betting Harbourside Local Area Command has given Paxton a heads up on the situation, just in case it gets more complicated. The kidnapping occurred in their area but seeing it involves a politician everyone's diving for cover. Seems our success rate when dealing with pollies will make us the chosen ones if anything does eventuate.'

'Yeah okay, but let's face it, we still haven't charged anyone with the murder of that polly down on Bondi Beach, you know, whatshisname?'

'You mean Robert Porter, the guy who was married to Louisa who is now Louisa Lee and working with hubby over at the Taipan Club?'

Noel nodded in recollection. 'That's right. At least we know it wasn't suicide as he had more holes in him than a golf course. To me that tends to suggest he upset someone.'

Simon rose from his chair and strolled slowly to the office's one and only window. Adjusting the venetian blind, he pondered the hideous but thought-provoking brick wall that confronted him before slowly returning to his chair. 'Yep, give me a simple murder any day as I can't say I've investigated too many kidnappings,' he said. 'Come to think of it, the last one was when I was in high school and Belarius kidnapped Cymbeline's two sons. Anyway, there wouldn't be too much investigating to be done, not with the ransom letter providing names and a return address. And only asking for a hundred bucks. Hell, either the kidnappers are totally off their rockers or they must think the victim looks like the north end of a south bound camel and wouldn't fetch a nickel in a pub raffle.'

'Aah, come on, boss. It's the odd politician who puts their better half before their egos. You only have to recall what Louisa Porter had to say about how her husband treated her before someone did her a favour and stuck him with a knife.'

Simon harrumphed. 'Yeah well, she should've known better than to marry what she did as opposed to who she did. At least she had the sense to leave him before someone did him in. But this thing with Blakey is a bit confusing. His wife's gone and got herself kidnapped, the kidnappers are demanding a nickel and dime ransom but Mr Blakey doesn't want her back at any price. On top of that, Mr Blakey doesn't want the police to take any action. Maybe Blakey might condescend to take her back if the kidnappers paid him or he might pay them to keep her.'

Having retrieved a scrap of paper from the waste paper bin next to his desk, Noel rolled it into a ball and had a three-point shot at Simon's similarly located bin – and missed; nothing unusual. 'Thing is,' he said, 'I think Mr Blakey is pushing the emotional barrow in order to gain sympathy from people in his electorate, not that I think he set up the kidnapping. While wishing to portray the happily married man, he obviously isn't losing any sleep over his loss, unless someone else is keeping him awake at night, that is. It seems he's happy to let everyone know his wife's been nicked and has even gone to the trouble to release a press statement advising of the kidnapping and that the police are conducting an exhaustive investigation into the matter, which is obviously a load of codswallop.'

Simon frowned in exasperation. 'Look, I know we've been directed not to investigate, but just for our own interest, we'll let the dust settle for a couple of days then go 'round to the kidnapper's place and have a quiet chat. I'd love to know what's going on even if Paxton and Fisher don't.'

━━━

'WELL, I'll be stuffed, if it's not Benny,' Simon exclaimed. 'I haven't seen you since you and Jacko were riding around on a Harley trying to intimidate people.'

'Yeah, back in the good old days, but your misses organised that and I was only doin' Jacko a favour who was doin' you a favour,' Benny responded with a smile. 'Anyway, you better come in. Alf's in the kitchen and I s'pose you want to talk to us about some ransom note we sent to a politician?'

'Thanks Benny, and you're right on that score,' Simon said as Benny led the two men down the hall and into the kitchen.

'Alf, we have a couple of detectives who'd like to have a chat about that note we sent to Mr Blakey,' Benny said as Alf pushed his chair back from the table and stood to greet the two detectives.

Following Benny's introductions, Alf, with a wave of the hand, invited the detectives to take a seat. 'Yeah, I s'pose we were expecting the coppers to call around eventually, even if we haven't done anything illegal,' he said with a tinge of reluctant acceptance of the inevitable.

'Oh, so you don't consider kidnapping a felony?' Noel asked presumptuously.

'Yeah, but a kidnapping is only a kidnapping if the kidnapee is taken against their wishes. If the person being kidnapped, the kidnapee, happens to ask the kidnappers to be kidnapped in the first place, that would make the victim one of the villains. And if the victim is also one of the villains, one cancels the other out and no crime has been committed,' Alf explained having spent many hours trying to work out the legal implications.

'You mean to tell me the whole thing was a scam?' Simon asked, somewhat surprised by Alf's revelation.

Alf, with an air of confidence, sat back and locked his hands together behind his head. 'Yep. Rosetta, that's the name of Mr Blakey's wife, wanted to fleece Mr Blakey for a stack of money and decided a kidnapping was the best way of doing it. She figured that would suit her financially and Mr Blakey politically, what with an election in twelve months' time. Don't get me wrong, there's no way in the world Rosetta would deliberately go out of her way to help her husband as she really dislikes the little sod. It's just that people might have some misguided belief that he's a good bloke and tend to feel sorry for him, especially if he appears grief-stricken by the event, which he wouldn't. I know, I know, politics and policies aside, there's a lot of people who would vote for him for no other reason than his wife had been involved in a kidnapping.'

Simon looked across the table to Noel who sat with a vacant look on his face. 'Come on, Noel, what are your thoughts on the matter?' Simon asked.

'Well, to start with, I had an inkling nothing was going to be simple, what with a politician who can't, or won't, find a hundred bucks to get his wife back from the clutches of some gangster gang. Blakey already told us back in Paxton's office that he's not fussed one way or the other if Rosetta is returned or not. Irrespective of the outcome, he has to at least give the impression he's doing all he can to recover his wife. It seems like we have the proverbial Mexican standoff. While Mr Blakey tries to convince the electorate he's Mr Nice Guy and what a great family man he is, Rosetta now has all she needs to expose the real domestic situation and that hubby thinks she's not worth any amount money, irrespective of how insignificant that amount may be. It's obvious he's out on the hustings already, probably enjoying himself, and doesn't want Mrs Rosetta back at any price.'

'And Alf, you had no idea Mr Blakey would renege on paying the ransom?' Simon asked.

Alf rocked back on his chair and pulled his bottom lip before replying. 'Chief Inspector, we had no idea who would do what. Jacko over at the Taipan Club gave me a phone call one day and asked if we could do one of the club's clients a favour. After meeting Rosetta, we said we would help as it wasn't a real kidnapping, seeing she was doing the planning. Whatever her domestic situation was wasn't any of our business and she didn't seem to have any doubt that Mr Blakey would pay her ransom. She said she wanted to screw him for a heap of money before she divorced him. Due to a misunderstanding in writing the ransom note, we asked for one hundred dollars for Rosetta's safe return. She didn't say anything about thousands when she said one hundred, so how was Benny or I to know she meant a hundred thousand? Gawd luv us, no-one's worth that much anyway.'

'So, at that time you were under the impression he would pay the one hundred dollars?' Noel asked.

'Well, if we thought he wouldn't cough up, Benny here wouldn't have put a return address on the envelope. He had to have some idea of where to send the money.'

Simon pressed his lips together, folded his arms and slowly shook his head. 'Okay, as I take it Rosetta was brought here after the kidnapping, just where is she now?'

'Wouldn't have a clue,' Alf replied. 'She seemed a bit upset with our ransom demand and was a little put out when Benny here told her he'd put a return address on the envelope. She packed a bag, rang for a taxi and took off expecting the police to arrive on the doorstep at any moment. Benny and I are still here because we've done nothing wrong as far as the police are concerned, at least we think, or hope so. All we had to do was convince Mr Blakey that his wife had been kidnapped and the kidnappers, me and Benny, were demanding money for her return. And we can't be kidnappers because I read it in a legal dictionary somewhere that to kidnap someone, the kidnapping must be without the victim's consent. In this case, the victim consented and even organised the event. And although we asked Mr Blakey for some money, there was no actual demand for the payment and there was never any threat of violence.'

As Simon and Noel left the small Chandos Street semi-detached bungalow, it was Noel who voiced the common thought of the two detectives. 'All I can say is that for once I'll be happy to agree with a politician. If Blakey's happy to let the investigation slide, I'm happy to comply with Fisher's orders and let it slide as well.'

Chapter 5

Simon sat at his desk and looked dejected, probably because he was. The traffic, even for the short distance from Crows Nest back to the city, had been diabolical and really, who cares if Rosetta had been genuinely kidnapped, he thought. 'I s'pose Alf is correct, if what he says is true. I mean, to charge someone with kidnapping, the kidnapping has to be done without the consent of the victim, and Rosetta was very much the consenting victim, at least according to Alf and Benny. The only person she was trying to convince it wasn't a set-up was hubby and he, apparently, couldn't care less.'

'Then what's the reason for Mr Blakey not wanting us to investigate?' Noel asked. 'It's not as though he's aware that the whole thing was a scam perpetrated by Rosetta.'

'Who knows? Maybe that's a question only Morton can answer,' Simon replied. 'Maybe an investigation would open up a can of worms that he would prefer to remain closed. Unfortunately for people in the public eye, there's any number of reasons they would prefer the general public to be kept in ignorance, like professional or personal misconduct over and above the call of that expected of a squeaky clean married member of society with whom the public have placed their trust.'

'Okay, so we've been told not to investigate the kidnapping that wasn't a kidnapping,' Noel said with a touch of indifference. 'We could always charge Rosetta with wasting police time, but then I doubt she would have considered the repercussions of her actions and had no intention of being a pain in the butt, at least not for the police. Anyway, I s'pose it's all water under the bridge now. No doubt all the politicians will be running around the streets in the not too distant future putting up photos of themselves while Morton Blakey's ever-loving wife has chosen to try and screw Mr Blakey's hide to the wall, if not his wallet.'

Before Simon could comment, their discussion on the Blakey's matrimonial issues was interrupted by the ringing of his phone which he promptly answered. After a quick exchange lasting no more than a few seconds, Simon replaced the receiver, pushed his chair back and, without saying a word, motioned to Noel; they had been summoned.

'And what's this all about?' Noel asked as they headed down the corridor.

'Haven't a clue,' Simon responded. 'Fisher wants to see us, that's all.'

Two quick knocks on the door provoked an immediate and hostile response. 'Enter, take a seat and don't interrupt.' It was obvious the annoyance currently afflicting Superintendent Fisher was about to be shared with the two detectives. 'Before I start, I want to know if you two dimwits have taken any action on that politician's stupid report of a kidnapping?'

'Apart from a visit to the two mental giants involved, no, sir,' Simon replied as he squirmed uncomfortably into his chair. 'Why, are we supposed to be investigating it?'

'No, not at all. And we really don't give a damn about the kidnapping. Mr Blakey had no involvement in that little incident and probably will have little involvement in any other incident,' Fisher said as he sat as his desk, a tormented look on his face.

'Oh, and why is that, sir? Is Blakey giving politics away?' Noel asked.

Fisher rocked back on his chair, his hands clasped on his stomach. 'Yes,' he said, slowing nodding his head, 'I think it's safe to say Blakey has already given politics away. In fact, I think Mr Blakey has given everything away. Seems he fell in front of a train at Town Hall Station.'

'You're joking?' came Simon's immediate response.

'Unfortunately, it's not a joking matter as the man's dead. I suggest you get yourselves up there right away. A crime scene has been established and that pathology bloke, Graham Gallymore, has been called in.'

'So, if Gally's been summoned there must be doubt that it was some sort of an accident?' Noel asked the stupidly superfluous question.

Superintendent Fisher glared. 'Sergeant Elliott, I'll ignore that as I'm sure Doctor Gallymore would not have been called in if it was a simple accident or a suicide. I'm short of details but there has to be some doubt as to the cause of death, apart from being hit by a train. The officer attending the scene called Gallymore in as there's suspicion of foul play. Now, DCI Webster, I suggest you get up to Town Hall and see what this is all about – and take your sergeant with you.'

⊏⊐

THE UNDERGROUND TOWN HALL STATION is a busy place at the best of times. However, with the unconventional and unexpected death of an awaiting commuter, and train timetables thrown into a state of melt-down, the busy station was transformed from busy to chaotic as irate passengers vented their spleen on the police and ambulance officers in attendance. While it could be argued there was a justifiable reason for some disruption to services, it was of little consequence to the masses who had a train to catch. As with any hiccup to the city infrastructure, let alone the sordid events causing the turmoil to train services, demands were promptly forthcoming from aggravated commuters for the immediate and concerted intervention by related union officialdom.

The electric train responsible for the commuter disaster had stopped about forty metres along the platform after exiting the tunnel, well short of its normal station stopping point. As a consequence, the majority of its carriages, together with is load of now bemused commuters were left, both literally and metaphorically, in the dark. Most of the activity appeared to be concentrated in the area in front of the first carriage where the train driver, currently in a state of shock and being attended to by ambulance personnel, might be expected to be located. Entry to the platform was being denied to the public by the constabulary, while those commuters wishing to leave the platform as quickly as possible, and there were hundreds of gobsmacked witnesses who preferred they weren't, were having their exodus likewise impeded by uniformed police and railway employees. Again, nothing is simple and the exiting hordes, anxious to find alternate and timely transport, were required to provide the strategically placed constables with their details and answer a few brief questions before departure, much to the chagrin of the multitude involved.

'Cripes,' Simon muttered as the two detectives descended the last few steps leading onto the platform, 'whoever did Blakey in, if he was done in, couldn't have picked a better spot. Sixty zillion witnesses and I bet no-one saw anything. Reminds me of the TV show where a young girl standing on the platform is heaved out in front of a train by a politician.'

'Oh yeah. I saw that. Pretty brutal but a very effective way to murder someone,' Noel replied as he squeezed through a dense flock of would-be commuters. 'There's Gally, over there near the edge of the platform,' he said pointing.

'Hi Gally,' greeted Simon as he interrupted Gally's discussion with a uniformed senior sergeant. 'So damned crowded down here, I'm surprised we haven't had people slide off the platform in front of a train more often.'

'So, this is what they mean by jumping to conclusions,' Noel commented.

Graham Gallymore smiled. 'Yeah, well, I have my doubts Mr Blakey had it in mind to intentionally collide with the 1530 to Milsons Point. And I'd say the chances of him accidently slipping off into oblivion are pretty remote.'

'You mean someone provided a little help for him to end up where he did?' Noel asked.

'Wouldn't surprise me. The body's in a bit of a mess at the moment so I won't be able to draw any firm conclusions until I put the pieces we have back in place. At least it will give me something to do over the weekend and I do love a good jigsaw.'

'That bad?' Simon queried with a surprised look. 'I've never seen a cadaver resulting from a hit by a train; cars and trucks, yes, but trains, nope. And no, I don't particularly want to see Mr Blakey. I presume that's him under the…'

'Yes, it is. And the poor old train driver doesn't look too good either, what with someone jumping out in front of him, even if he was slowing down. Can we….?' Gally asked tentatively and indicated to the blue wrapped bundle on the platform.

'Sure, the sooner the better,' Simon responded. 'One hell of a way to commit murder, if it is murder. And with Blakey being a politician we won't be short of suspects. I wonder if his ever-loving wife was on the platform at the time.'

'Sorry Simon, that's your problem. I'll e-mail you a preliminary report on the outcome of my poking around which should be in a couple of days. Okay, boys, take it away,' Gally ordered his two white coated assistants.

Chapter 6

Simon Webster was a frustrated detective chief inspector and the suspicious death of a state politician in his bailiwick did nothing to allay his frustration. 'Tell me, Noel, why in the world do politicians seem to think they have to be the centre of attention when really no-one gives a damn? I bet you can't give me the name of the state Premier or even one of his ministers.'

At the other end of the office, Noel picked up a pen and unconsciously fiddled with it while, with a look of intense concentration, he considered Simon's speculative assertion. 'Nope, I'll concede you that one. I haven't a clue who's who in state politics and my knowledge of federal politics isn't much better. Politicians haven't enough longevity in the job before they commit some diabolical act of sheer stupidity and get kicked out before the people get to know them. But that's beside the point. We have a dead body and, as we've been directed to have a look at the situation, we should proceed on the assumption we have a murder victim.'

'Yeah, okay,' Simon conceded. 'I s'pose you're right but I may as well get a permanent office next to the Premier's. I'll have to go and have a chat with him, whoever the Premier happens to be at the moment.'

Noel sat back on his chair, the fiddling of the pen now given way to his annoying habit of clicking the retractable point. 'Well, I view the current flock of pollies an ephemeral lot more concerned with gravy train benefits they can scrounge from their position of supposed trust and honesty before the electorate gets wise and gives them the shove. It doesn't raise a mention in the newspapers when some polly gets kicked out for some nefarious activity, such as accepting an undisclosed donation from a foreign company or a bribe from a developer wanting a prime piece of real estate.

'But don't get me going as we're supposed to be apolitical, irrespective of what political inclinations you may have. Now, if I can get off my soapbox we'll draw up some sort of a collection plan as to who might have killed Morton Blakey, if someone did do him in. And seeing we're talking about who could have terminated a politician, we could be here 'till doomsday.'

Simon rested his cheek in the palm of his hand and tapped the side of his face with his fingers. 'Okay, Rosetta Blakey's name must be at the head of the list and I suppose Alf's and Benny's names should be included, not that I think they could be expected to have a motive. You'd better write these down on the whiteboard as I have a hunch the list will expand considerably once I've spoken to the Premier.'

'And you think he might be able to give you a few clues as to what's going on?' Noel enquired, acknowledging that with Simon's prickly relationship with the previous state Premier, he would be lucky to survive little longer than the introduction.

Simon shrugged and looked pensive. 'Look, after the last Premier was forced to resign because of that Elizabeth Bay mansion affair, I probably won't make it into his office. On top of that, as I haven't a clue what political party Blakey represents, or should I say represented, I'll have to rely on the Premier to bring me up to speed with the goings on in Macquarie Street.'

Noel selected a black marker from his desk drawer, heaved himself out of his chair and proceeded to drag the whiteboard to the middle of the office where, in large printing, he wrote the name "Morton BLAKEY" in the centre of the board. 'I know it's early days and we don't know if we have a murder to investigate, but maybe a priority should be to find Rosetta. After all, she thinks her husband is a worm and wants to divorce him. Maybe she got the idea that bumping him off would be a lot quicker, save a lot of rigmarole and the cost of an expensive divorce. And I apologise for my tautology as there's no such thing as a cheap divorce.'

Simon harrumphed. 'Look, according to Alf, Rosetta got the idea of a kidnapping from her girlfriends up at the Taipan Club and we know the lovely Louisa had a hand in it. It's a good enough excuse for a social get-together on the back lawn to discuss whatever's going on, not that we need an excuse. And in any case, it's about time we caught up socially with Graham and Louisa.' Although the Taipan Club was an illegal casino, Graham had maintained close rapport with the police and provided a constant and valued supply of information relating to Sydney's underworld activities. As a consequence, the Lees and the Websters had forged a sound friendship that extended to other Webster companions.

Whatever thoughts the detectives may have been contemplating regarding the future investigation into the death, accidental or otherwise of Morton Blakey, such thoughts were interrupted by Simon's phone. After a fairly lengthy one-sided discussion, punctuated by Simon's occasional "yes, I see, no", he hung up and did two three sixties on his battered office chair before halting his rotations. Folding his arms, he looked at Noel at the other end of the office with a serious look on his face.

Noel shook his head in disappointment. 'Don't tell me. That was the lottery office just to tell you, you didn't win, again.'

'No, that wasn't the bloody lottery office; it was Gally. Now, do you want the short or long version?' the detective chief inspector responded tersely.

'Okay, keep your shirt on. I'll have the long version.'

'No, you won't, too complicated. All you need to know is that our Mr Blakey was stabbed in the back before being thrown in front of the train.'

'Accidental?'

'Have my doubts.'

'So, he was murdered?'

'As I have grave reservations on the suicide angle, murder comes up as a distinct possibility,' Simon responded. 'Someone was well aware that a stab in the back is part of the normal daily routine and an occupational hazard for a politician. As the someone, who obviously knew this, needed to make sure Mr Blakey was going to end up dead, the someone incorporated some other additional means to ensure the successful passing on of our illustrious politician.'

'And the train was the other additional means?'

Simon rested his elbow on his desk and nibbled his little finger nail. After considering Noel's in-depth question, he responded. 'Gally can't say for sure whether the train was needed or not although he thinks the stab wound probably wasn't fatal. Doesn't really matter as the end result was still the same.'

'So, best you let Fisher know we have a murder investigation on our hands. At least that will keep him off our back for a while,' Noel said.

Chapter 7

It seemed the novelty of having a quiet drink on the back lawn of Simon's Collaroy bungalow while in the company of good friends would never cease. Being a stone's throw from the beach, a fact not lost on a peckish sea-going intruder, the unpleasant hot summer mornings usually gave way to a cooling afternoon sea breeze making conditions at 24 West Bank Lane perfect for a congenial afternoon get-together. Simon had arranged the half dozen director chairs around a small garden table on a carefully groomed back yard lawn in readiness for his guests. On the table, Georgie, Simon's wife, had placed an arrangement of assorted nibblies, a mandatory requirement while savouring a delicate chardonnay or the occasional can of the light amber, together with other para-phernalia needed for a social gathering.

Georgie was a tall, slim, short haired brunette with an olive completion and deep brown eyes. Despite the fact that she was married to a detective chief inspector, she had firmly established herself within the closely-knit group of friends as somewhat of a homicidal maniac having herself been directly responsible for the untimely death of the next-door neighbour, Dorothy. That Dorothy had been an arachnophobe had been considered by the coroner as a contributing factor after Dorothy had been found dead of a heart attack, the cause being attributed to the sight of a huntsman spider in her peg basket. While Georgie, who held very little fondness for the cantankerous old cow, was well aware of Dorothy's aversion to creepy crawlies, she had failed to consider the possible repercussions or likely outcome of placing the already dead huntsman, albeit a fairly large and intimidating looking specimen even when dead, in the basket. And to be honest, how was Georgie to know her simple act would have such unintended consequences, at least for Dorothy.

HAVING DISCUSSED the general run of the mill subjects such as the weather, politics, football and Holden cars, it was Simon who eventually broached the more sensitive issues of murder and kidnapping. With both Graham and Louisa Lee currently enjoying a dose of Webster hospitality, Simon felt the direct approach, as opposed to beating around the bush, might elicit a more favourable reception and negate the possibility of some awkward questions.

'And Louisa, I believe you have acquainted a girlfriend to the trials and tribulations of being married to a politician?'

Before answering, the vivacious brunette cast her hazel eyes upon Simon and gave a hint of a smile. 'Well, if anyone is qualified to give that sort of advice, I would say I was that person, having been married to one for too long. But the short answer to your question is, yes. Rosetta Blakey was aware of my history and asked if I had any ideas on how to make life as uncomfortable for her husband as he was making hers. And the answer to your next question is an emphatic, no, murder was not one of the ideas.'

Noel, who had been eavesdropping on the conversation,

butted in. 'And Louisa, have you any idea where Rosetta is at the moment?'

'Yes.'

'Well?' Simon asked somewhat perplexed. 'Despite your conviction that she didn't stab hubby in the back then push him under a train just to make sure he was dead, doesn't alter the fact that we would like to have a chat with the lady at some point.'

'No, I suppose you have a job to do and you'll find out sooner or later anyway. Rosetta is shacked up on *Gemini*.'

'Holy hell, who said she could?' the tall, lean and dark-haired man dressed in blue slacks and a white polo top, intervened.

'Sorry love, but after she discovered her kidnappers had included a return address on the ransom note, she had a premonition that things might not work out as planned. Taking a pragmatic view of the situation, the thought of staying at Crows Nest didn't seem such a good idea, so she left. As she needed somewhere to stay, and that somewhere wasn't at home with Morton who apparently doesn't think she's worth a plugged nickel, I suggested *Gemini*.' Anyway, Charlie said he'd look after her.' Charlie was Charles Chambers, considered by all to be a good bloke employed as the permanent deck hand on *Gemini*, Graham's fifty-five foot flybridge cruiser moored at Rushcutter Bay on Sydney Harbour.

Turning to Simon, Graham asked, 'So I s'pose you'll want to go and have a chat with her?'

'No, we won't go racing off to see her before we have some answers,' Simon, who had a preference of knowing the answer to a question before asking it, responded. 'As long as you're happy to let her remain where she is, Graham, I'd rather leave her alone for the present. After all, it's not as though she's guilty of anything - I think. Ron, do you know anything about Morton Blakey, apart from the fact he was a politician and is now a dead politician?'

The question was addressed to Ron Lange, a rather short, tubby man who, by circumstances beyond his control, had become a police informer and currently in the process of pouring a chardonnay for his girlfriend, Judy Kemp. Judy, a strong looking red head with a cluster of freckles around her nose, owned the next door premises at 26 West Bank Lane while choosing to live with Ron in Sydney's eastern suburbs and rent out the Collaroy home. 'What, you're asking me about a politician?' Ron replied rather indignantly. 'Know nothing, but if he was stabbed in the back, I'd put my money on some other politician having planted the dirk.'

Simon lobbed his empty beer can into the metal garbage bin specifically designated as the receptacle for the tossing of empty beer cans before rummaging around in the esky and extracting two more coldies, one of which he passed to Ron. 'Okay people, is there anyone here who knows anything about Mr Blakey at all, apart from the obvious?'

It was the blue eyed blond girl who, after leaning forward and placing her wine glass on the table, volunteered what she knew of Morton Blakey. Sue was Noel's wife and, due to circumstances emanating from the close professional relation-ship of the four men currently sitting around the garden table, a cordial social coterie had evolved between Louisa, Georgie, Judy and Sue. As it transpired, discussions within the group tended to focus on matters currently under investigation by their men-folk. The girls were often able to contribute from a purely objective point of view and provide a unique perspec-tive on issues being aired based on those unique attributes unavailable to the mere male gender of female logic, intuition and the female imagination.

'Yes, I seem to remember reading something in the news-paper a few days ago,' Sue said. 'Blakey is a member of the governing party and when the Premier introduced a bill into the assembly that Blakey didn't agree with, Blakey crossed the floor and voted with the opposition. Apparently it was his vote that was enough to have the bill rejected, the government only holding a slim majority at the best of times. Naturally this went over like a lead balloon as it wasn't the first time Blakey had crossed the floor.'

Simon pursed his lips, lifted his eyebrows and nodded in acknowledgement. 'And you don't happen to know what the bill was about, do you?'

Sue shook her head. 'Come on, Simon. I just happened to glance at the paper. Whoever reads those bits about politics and parliament?'

'Okay, people,' Simon said as he squeezed the life out of the empty beer can before consigning it to the bin, 'the only person of interest, so far, is Rosetta whom I doubt would go from appropriating a few dollars from hubby to murdering him. However, it seems Blakey has managed to get a lot of people, including the Premier, off side. Ron, I want you to find out what you can about Blakey, his electorate and his staff members, if he has any. Graham, if you don't have any objections, I would like to ask Louisa to keep a friendly eye on Rosetta, you know, just have the occasional chit-chat to see if anything is forthcoming.'

'No, I've no problems with that but you'd better ask Louisa,' Graham replied as he took a handful of salted peanuts from the table.

'Louisa?'

'I haven't any objections even though I might feel like Mata Hari.'

'Good,' Simon replied. 'Ron, you happy to do a little searching?'

Ron shrugged and pressed his lips together. 'Yeah, I've always wanted an excuse to dig up stuff on a polly as the possibilities of what you may find are endless.'

'And you ain't whistlin' Dixie there, Ron,' Simon

responded. 'And Noel, as Rosetta is our only suspect at the moment, I want you to get over to the Registry of Births, Deaths and Marriages and see if you can get some background info on Mrs Blakey.'

'No problems, boss.'

'Right, I think that just about covers it. All I have to do is check with the Premier's office and find out if Blakey had gone out of his way to provide some disgruntled pleb a motive to do him a permanent mischief. Now, with all that out of the way, I think it's a good time for a bit of serious socializing and a few more coldies.'

Chapter 8

On arrival at the towering State Office Block, Simon was pleasantly surprised to see that the fashion-conscious receptionist he had met on previous visits to the building was the same fashion-conscious receptionist, albeit with some minor alterations, confronting him at the information desk. The pink mohawk hairstyle had given way to a short cut pageboy style that looked quite neat, if not a little garish, for the deep purple colour didn't seem to compliment the black lipstick and matching eye make-up.

The unidentifiable tattoo on the girl's right shoulder was now balanced with a similar unidentifiable tattoo on her left shoulder, both tattoos obviously having some esoteric meaning of which Simon had no burning desire to become aware of. While the silver stud that still protruded from her nose managed to provide Simon with a degree of fashion uncertainty, the thought of wearing a similar impediment to the life-saving function of breathing had never crossed his mind. While in total ignorance of the current trends in the younger generation's fashion consciousness, Simon had to concede the overall effect did contribute to the general charm and elegance of the young girl.

Dressed in mufti, Simon was taken aback somewhat when the damsel with the purple hair greeted him. 'Oh, hi there. You're the policeman who used to come around to see the old Premier, Mr Buckmaster,' she said with unexpected cheerfulness.

'Yes, that's right. Detective Chief Inspector Simon Webster. And you're…?'

'Jacqueline, but everybody calls me Jacky. Seeing we've seen so much of each other, you can call me Jacky. I'll still have to refer to you as "sir" as it's company policy.'

'No, that's fine, as long as you don't mind me calling you Jacky.'

'No, that'll be awesome. But you didn't come here to chat me up, so what can I do for you?'

Simon raised his eyebrows and replied questioningly. 'I'd like to have a brief word with the Premier who, I believe, is a Mr. Fortescue, a Mr Clyde Fortescue?'

'Yes, that's right. He hasn't been here long. It seems Mr Buckmaster had a few problems around the time you were visiting him, not that your visits could ever have had anything to do with his resignation. I have no idea what these Premiers get up to, but they never seem to last very long,' Jacky replied as she picked up an internal phone and, following a brief conversation, turned to Simon. 'You know the way, thirty ninth floor, turn right.'

'Yeah, thanks,' replied Simon as he headed for the express lift that would carry him non-stop to the Premier's office.

━━

PREMIER CLYDE FORTESQUE pushed his chair back from the ornate office table and stood as Lorraine, the Premier's tall red headed secretary, ushered Simon into the office. It was the Premier's office table that provided Simon with his first hint as to the character of the Premier. Simon was of the firm belief that the size of the table is, generally, directly proportional to the ego that sits behind it and, in this case, the Premier's table was big.

'Detective Chief Inspector Webster, I believe,' the Premier said as he rounded the table, his hand extended.

'Yes, that's right,' returned Simon as he took the Premier's hand while, at the same time, making an initial assessment as to whether he liked the man or not; he didn't.

'Please, take a seat. I believe you want to talk about Morton Blakey's death,' the Premier said as he indicated to four lounge chairs nestled around a coffee table in the centre of the room.

'Yes, I seem to recall he was a member of your back-benches and a person prone to cross the floor, which he seems to have done on a number of occasions,' Simon replied as he sank back in the plush leather chair.

'Yes, he could be a real pain in the butt. He was one of these altruistic idiots who believe it to be their democratic right to be guided by their conscience which was, on this latest occasion, totally contrary to party policy. Fortunately we have sufficient numbers in the Lower House to suffer such hiccups, sometimes. I've often tried to get him to see reason on some major issues, but it's as they say, you win some and you lose some,' replied Premier Fortescue.

'And can you tell me what this latest incident involved?'

Premier Fortesque gave an inconsequential shrug. 'It was just a minor matter relating to an overseas investment, nothing of any significance but something we want to get through parliament.'

'Can you tell me something about the man, you know, what was he like as an individual, discounting the fact that he was a politician?' Simon asked, dispensing with any form of political correctness.

'Unfortunately, Blakey was an uneducated buffoon lacking any charm or charisma. The man was devoid of even a smattering of common sense and totally incapable of coming to grips with the nuts and bolts of government business or party strategy.' At this point the Premier paused for a moment of reflection. 'Come to think of it, I suppose it can only be expected of one from the lower classes. The man came from one of those government run combined high schools and no-one with any potential or aptitude comes from those schools. You see, Chief Inspector Webster, there are essential natural character traits required to be a politician and these character-istics are normally endowed only by those of the elite who can afford an education commensurate with their status within the community.'

Having visualised a silver spoon hanging from the Premier's mouth, Simon nodded in acknowledgement. 'I'll remember that, especially as I come from Manly Boys' High which is one of the government's combined high schools of the lower classes to which you refer. I take it you were educated at Grammar, maybe Scots College?'

'Grammar, of course, then a five year law degree at Cambridge before returning to Australia.'

'How nice,' replied Simon. 'I did year twelve then two years at the police academy out in the sticks at Goulburn. And before you became Premier, I suppose you were a barrister, merchant banker or a rich property developer?'

'No, no, no, chief inspector. As I come from a very wealthy family, I've never had reason to work or associate with people of the lesser classes.'

Simon raised is eyebrows questioningly. 'You mentioned Mr Blakey was not one of the intellectual hierarchy and needed some learned counselling at times?'

The Premier harrumphed. 'Blakey was a good example of what I was referring to. The constituents out in the electorates haven't a clue. All a political candidate has to do is stand up on his soapbox, spin a few promises that sound too good to be true, and usually are, and the whacko voters will vote him, or her, into parliament.

'In all reality, the people in the electorate are unable to understand what it is that's best for themselves. It is us, the educated intellectuals, who have the responsibility to do the thinking for them and, as I was borne into the hierarchy, I am one of those people. We have taken on the burden, at great personal cost, of assessing what is best for the majority and to ensure whatever it is we think best is applied. Unfortunately, Mr Blakey was a square peg in a round hole and didn't have a clue just what side his bread was buttered. There were times when I had to take him aside and have a quiet word, just to get him on the same page.'

Simon reclined back in his expensive leather chair, crossed his legs at the ankle and folded his arms. 'Well, I'm sure Mr Morton Blakey would consider that whatever you assessed as being in his best interest was a bit wide of the mark, seeing he's dead.'

'Mr Blakey's death, Chief Inspector, was beyond my control. He was a man who rubbed a lot of people up the wrong way and was definitely not on top of the popularity list of many politicians, or plebs. Being a loose cannon, he made a lot of enemies in the political world as you could never rely on his support to get a bill through the House. Heaven knows how he ever won pre-selection and got himself elected. I'm not one to speak ill of the dead, but someone did us all a big favour by getting rid of the obnoxious little buffoon even if it comes down to a bi-election for his seat, which it won't considering the circumstances of his death.'

'Apart from a multitude of people wanting to murder the buffoon, is there anyone who comes to mind who you think might have had the propensity to carry out the deed?' Simon asked.

Premier Fortesque contemplated the question for a

moment before replying. 'Yes, I could probably name a few politicians who have had their nose put out of joint, but I very much doubt they'd resort to murder. However, I do know of at least one non-politician who might have harboured such extreme thoughts. I dare say you'll find out sooner than later so I may as well let you know now. We have some foreign interest in a particular piece of real estate with a Mr David Zheng heading up a Hong Kong based consortium wishing to build a six-star hotel on the land. No doubt Mr Blakey's little gimmick of crossing the floor to have my Foreign Ownership Bill defeated wouldn't have gone over too well with Mr Zheng.'

'And you think this Mr Zheng might have the inclination to eliminate anyone who gets up his nose?' Simon asked, his curiosity piqued with the introduction of a new name.'

'DCI Webster, although my relationship with Mr Zheng have been quite limited, I have found him to be a man of integrity and honesty. I would be greatly surprised if he had the inclination to kill time.'

'And the property Mr Zheng is so zealously anxious to acquire?'

'The owner of an illegal gambling casino here in the city is considering closing it down. Obviously we are anxious that the post-sale future of the property is handled in a manner that will be looked upon as a fine example of what can be achieved with the appropriate intervention and close collaboration by those within the decision making elements of society, and the relevant property developers, of course.'

Aah yes, the relationship between the inimitable politician and the inimical developer, Simon thought sarcastically. 'And the name of the casino?' Simon asked, his faith in those within the decision-making elements of society rapidly sinking to a new low.

The Premier gave a wry smile. 'Why, it's the Taipan Club of course, which I believe is owned by your friend Graham Lee. Anyway, getting back to your investigation and the reason for your visit, I believe Mr Blakey was stabbed in the back before being shunted under a train?'

After a few seconds of bemused silence following the Premier's display of egotistical self-confidence, Simon vaguely answered the Premier's question, 'that's right, stabbed in the back and pushed in front of a train.'

'You don't think the stabbing could have been a symbolic gesture? Most politicians get stabbed in the back once or twice in their careers, metaphorically speaking of course,' Fortesque queried having decided he could afford to adopt a smug attitude having delivered a curved ball to the Detective Chief Inspector.

'I doubt there's anything symbolic in getting hit by a train, but you think one of your political associates might have taken the extra step and decided to have a go literally?' Simon asked, having relegated the information on Graham Lee to its required mental pigeon hole.

'Well, for all the metaphorical backstabbing of politicians I've seen go on in parliament, I would think a politician must be high on the list of suspects. By the same token, I have heard that Morton and Rosetta, his wife, didn't get on too well together. Maybe she did the job. I know Morton was never averse to a bit on the side, and if Rosetta got wind of it, who knows?'

'Anyone in particular?' Simon asked with an enquiring look.

'Naturally there was a close working relationship with his campaign manager who just happens to be a strikingly good-looking woman, not that there is anything to suggest there was anything more to it than what it was, or supposed to have been. Her name's Jezebel Dawkins, if that's any help to you.'

Simon twitched his head to acknowledge the possibility. 'Yep, she might be. And as they say, hell hath no fury like a woman scorned.'

'Amen to that.'

Simon paused for a moment before folding his arms. 'You know, Mr Premier, this is the second murder of a politician within the last couple of years. I can't help thinking that their rate of planetary departure may be somewhat inconsistent with that which might be expected from within a vocation regarded by most as not being physically, or mentally, demanding.'

Obviously having hit a raw nerve, the Premier rose from his chair and, with great difficulty maintaining his composure, returned to his desk, his affable countenance now one of aggrieved displeasure. 'Chief Inspector Webster, the decision-making process within parliament is an onerous and painstaking task, the outcome of which will not necessarily be amenable to all within the community. If it were, we would not need an opposition or an Upper House; everyone would be happy with every decision.'

'So, you're saying all decisions are based on what is considered best for the majority of the community while there are those who will be aggrieved by such decisions?' Simon returned it what had now developed into a hostile exchange.

'Of course.'

'And money has no influence over any decision-making process?'

'Chief inspector, I refuse to lower myself to even give your question consideration.'

Simon raised his eyebrows, pressed his lips tightly together and nodded. 'Well, damned if I know how developers can get approval to dig up state owned crown land, which is unavailable to the plebs, and build unsightly housing developments on the harbour foreshore. Yep, beats me.'

Chapter 9

Rosetta Blakey might be the vindictive wife with a defective imagination. However, whether she was capable of dreaming up a scurrilous plan to do her husband terminal mischief, irrespective of the fact that hubby might well be a philandering sod, as claimed by the Premier and deserved whatever he got, was open to speculation and a matter yet to be substantiated. Would she go so far as to murder the target of her unforgiving vengeance when her expressed aim was solely to fleece some money out of her half-wit husband and make his life miserable; not go to the extreme and shunt him off the planet in an act of unmitigated hatred?

So, a politician had been done away. Given a choice, Simon would rather investigate the effects of global warming on the sale of sun tan lotion, or the impact of increased petrol pricing on the push-bike market. In fact, there was little Simon wouldn't do to avoid having to conduct an investigation into the premature passing of a perverse politician. However, notwithstanding Simon's tendency to display some degree of antipathy towards those exhibiting an ego fostered elitism, Simon was a cop with a job to do, and the fact that the victim in this case just happened to be a politician was beside the point. Oh, well, best I get on with it, Simon thought.

━━━

ALTHOUGH THE TAIPAN Club was closed for business, it being mid-morning, Jacko welcomed Simon to the casino with a broad smile. 'I guess you've come to see Mr Lee,' the gentle giant doorman said as he ushered Simon from the footpath and into the casino.

'Well, yes, Jacko, but I would like a word with you too, if you don't mind. The boss in?'

'Yeah, he's expectin' you. You know where his office is.'

'Thanks, Jacko, but to save on a bit of repetition I think you should come along too.'

Jacko nodded and gave a slight shrug. 'Sure thing, although I can't see why you should need me. I've been straight since last time,' Jacko said with a wry smile.

The door to Graham Lee's office was open, the owner of the Taipan Club lounging in a relaxed manner in his office chair located behind a mahogany desk on which his feet, crossed at the ankles, rested, a small glass of scotch whisky in his hand.

'Cripes, the sun ain't over the yardarm yet and you're already into it,' came Simon's response at seeing his long-time friend reposed in such a seemingly relaxed manner. 'Something must be wrong somewhere?'

'Seems so, unfortunately, but I won't bore you with the details at the moment. Care to join me?' Graham asked as he rose from his desk to re-establish himself on a three-seater lounge located in front of an enormous wall-mounted TV set.

'A tad early for me, and I am working,' Simon replied as he settled himself on a matching lounge chair. Jacko gave an enquiring look to his boss before he, too, occupied the remaining lounge chair. Although Simon was on official duty, the office was devoid of any tension or unease, probably due to the fact that Simon and Graham, along with their respective spouses, shared both an amicable professional and social friendship.

Jacko, on the other hand, circulated in a different socio-economic environment. Notwithstanding, he had known Simon for years and had become well acquainted after a somewhat inauspicious introduction when Simon and Noel had encountered Jacko in the process of trying to rob a hotel down in The Rocks area of Sydney. In fact, it was Benny who had been in cahoots with Jacko when they tried to plunder the hotel of its alcoholic beverages.

'And what exactly is the purpose of your visit to the Taipan Club, Simon?' Graham asked as leaned forward and placed his empty glass on the coffee table.

'Sort of a long story which I won't go into. However, the short version of it is I'm investigating the murder of the politician, or ex politician, Morton Blakey, you know, the bloke who got himself run over by a train.'

'Aah, yes. We talked about him out on your back lawn.' Graham replied with a nod of the head. 'But as I can't say I've ever met the bloke, or even having seen him. What's he got to do with me?'

'Probably nothing although Jacko here may be able to shed some light on the subject. Jacko, it seems you helped Rosetta Blakey with some problem she had. We believe you provided Mrs Blakey with the name and phone number of someone you thought might be able to provide the specific assistance she needed.'

Jacko frowned and shook his head. 'Sorry, boss,' Jacko said with an appealing look to Graham, 'but Mrs Lee, who is a friend of Rosetta Blakey through Rosetta's attendance at the club, asked if I could help out with a problem Rosetta had. All I did was arrange for Rosetta to get in touch with Benny. You know, Benny on the motor bike and from that pub heist that went wrong.'

'It's okay, Jacko. We've already been to see Benny and you've done nothing wrong,' Simon reassured Jacko with a smile.

Having confirmed Benny's story of events with Jacko, Simon sat back and turned to Graham. 'Getting right off the subject, Graham, I hear on the grape-vine the club is going to be knocked down for a high-rise residential complex.'

'That's right, or at least that was the idea, hence my problem,' Graham replied as he rose and returned to his desk. 'My early splicing of the mainbrace may have something to do with the hiccups I now foresee on the horizon. Maybe I'd better explain,' he said and, after refilling his glass from a bottle in the top drawer of his desk, regained his office chair. 'After considering all options, I decided there were better long-term financial opportunities to guarantee a future income than to just sell off the club. The idea was to virtually give the property to a specific developer, with whom I've already had a few discussions. With the property in his name, or his company's name, he would have the security for a loan from a bank for construction of the complex.'

'Can you give me a name?' Simon asked tentatively.

'Sure. Glover Property Development over in Bondi. However, some overseas conglomerate with their own ideas as to what should happen to the place got wind of the deal and are talking about a plush six-star hotel. Anyway, they couldn't make a move without some political support, which is the current position at this moment. I should have known it wasn't going to be simple if it involved developers and politicians,' Graham said as he gulped the last of his Jonny Walker Black Label.

Simon thought for a moment with a look of deep concentration. 'I know it's a long shot, Graham, but have you given any thought that your problem may be connected to my problem in any way?'

'You mean the death of this backbench character?'

'Yep. Seems he had the propensity of getting people off side, including the Premier. He recently crossed the floor and voted with the opposition to defeat the Premier's bill relating to overseas ownership of a piece of Sydney's real estate. Seems these overseas hustlers aren't interested in investing but want to buy as much of the country as we'll let them, which amounts to about all of it. Strange,' Simon added after a moment mulling over the coincidence.

'In answer to your question, no I haven't, but nothing's beyond the bounds of probability, especially when dealing with politicians, developers and dead bodies,' Graham responded.

'And that's the point,' Simon remarked. 'Although we have a number of suspects, all female at the moment, I've this gut feeling a shonky involving the Premier, or one of his cronies, and a property developer, is just around the corner. Next time I see the Premier I'll make some discrete enquiries. I s'pose we all have our problems and all I have to worry about is the murder of some half-wit politician, which leads me to ask a favour. I'm delaying questioning Rosetta for the moment, but the time will come when we will need to have a chat. Any objections to my boarding *Gemini*?'

'No. None at all. Charlie's doing some work on one of the pumps, so *Gemini* isn't going anywhere for a while.'

As Simon rose to leave, he paused before turning to Graham. 'By the way, Graham, have you come across a man by the name of David Zheng?'

'Yeah, I believe he's heading up this overseas push for the club.'

Chapter 10

While seated, Simon shuffled his rickety chair closer to his desk and picked up a pen in preparation to write down details of Noel's and Ron's forthcoming tidings. 'Okay Ron, what have we got?'

Ron, casually sitting on top of a two drawer filing cabinet, withdrew a tattered notebook from his coat pocket. After a brief search and referring to the required entry, he raised his eyebrows and took a deep breath before replying. 'Ah, yes, Blakey has, or had, an office, well, sort of an office in Neutral Bay. I took a trip over and found it more of a broom closet than an office located in the basement of an office building. No-one was home but the sign on the door gave a telephone number for Blakey and one for Jezebel Dawkins, Blakey's old campaign manager, or should I say last campaign manager as I don't think Jezebel could be called old.

'I chased up Jezebel's number, found an address and went to see her. The address was that of Gem Development over at North Sydney where the CEO just happens to be a Mr Daniel Dawkins, who looks either like the successful businessman, or a pimp with all sorts of jewellery hanging off him. Mrs Dawkins is a strikingly beautiful lady; tall, long black hair and hazel eyes, and also works for Gem Development although I haven't quite worked out in what capacity. Both of them were aware of Morton's death but neither seemed unduly perturbed about the loss. They confirmed each other's alibi for the day Blakey snuffed it despite the fact that when I put the question to the receptionist on my way out she couldn't actually recall having seen either of them on that particular day. She did say that that was not unusual as they both seemed to be in and out of the office throughout the day. I intend following up on Gem Development, if for no other reason than to placate your aversion to property developers and the fact that the Dawkins are too smooth for my liking, not that they appeared to share any affinity for each other.'

Simon nodded his head in approval. 'Yes, that's a good idea. Every time a developer raises his head, a politician's head is going to pop out of the woodwork sooner or later, and Jezebel and Morton seem pretty close to the coalface. Thanks, Ron, that gives us a good start. Now Noel, what have you uncovered?'

Noel pushed his chair back from his desk, clenched his hands together on his lap and arched his thumbs. 'Well, if I hadn't have had anything in particular to do, I could've spent the whole day chasing up my own family records. The things you find at B, D and M. Anyway, it seems Rosetta Blakey was initially married to a bloke named Alvin Stone who just happened to be a backbencher during the Alex Martin period of Premiership; you know, Wally Ackerman was his deputy. Her occupation at that time was personal secretary to the Honourable Peter Mason, the Minister for Sport. The marriage ended when Alvin slipped over a cliff at Bradleys Head, not that the cliffs over there are very big but you can kill yourself slipping on a banana peel. I didn't have time to chase up everything I wanted to so I'll go back tomorrow and see if there's anything strange about the Dawkins.'

'And the water gets murkier,' Simon said with a frown and

a shake of the head. 'We have Jezebel, who is, or was, the campaign manager of a polly while at the same time married to a developer. Now, tell me there isn't a conflict of interest there somewhere. Everything seems to have turned out rather serendipitous for Rosetta, having made the same mistake twice by marrying a politician. She might have decided she wouldn't get much of a trade in on Alvin for a later model and Morton appears to have been about as popular as a dose of haemorrhoids. No, the redoubtable Rosetta Stone wanted to get rid of both of them, by fair means or foul. Eventually, by some means or other, she got lucky; hubby number one going over a cliff and number two having someone stick a knife in his back and throw him into the path of an on-coming train, which certainly did the trick.

'And although we're talking about the rage of women scorned, I think we have a developing crisis with Graham Lee's idea for an inner-city residential complex. While it sounds simple, it seems headed for the gurgler with an overseas conglomerate wishing to cash in on Sydney's lucrative tourist market with a new you-beaut hotel, which means someone has to be getting a kick-back, and no prizes for guessing who.'

'Yeah, but Graham's problem probably hasn't anything to do with the death of some backbencher,' Noel commented brusquely.

Simon, having decided he didn't need to take notes, tossed his pen onto the desk and leant back. 'I'm not so sure you're right on that score, Noel. You can call me a sceptic, but when it comes to politicians, anyone who thinks they're kosher has to be delusional. I'm not saying Graham's problem and the Blakey incident are connected, but so far we already have a flamboyant property developer, three dead politicians, one having been run over by a train, one falling over a cliff and another being hacked to death on Bondi Beach. Throw in a Premier I wouldn't trust as far as I could throw him and we have all the ingrediencies needed to make Titus Andronicus's pie look like a culinary delight. Noel, before you go over to B, D and M to check out the Dawkins duo, get over to Alf and Benny. See if they can recall anything unusual during Rosetta's stay with them. In the meantime, Ron, can you check the records on the death of the chipmunk, what was his name, Alvin someone or other?'

Ron smiled and nodded. 'The chipmunk was Alvin Stone, who probably wished he had been a chipmunk instead of dead at the bottom of a cliff. Mind you, Bradleys Head is probably one of the nicer places to depart this planet, if you have a choice of a departure point. And while Noel and I are doing all the footwork, what will you be doing?'

'Unless anyone else cares to volunteer, I propose to make a social call on our Premier.'

Chapter 11

'Hi, Jackie. The boss in today?' Simon asked in a somewhat flippant manner, a manner in which Jackie probably appreciated in preference to the long-winded demands of agitated pelicans who didn't know who, or what, they wanted in the first place.

'And good morning to you too, sir,' came Jackie's immediate glib response. 'As I presume you are referring to the Premier, the short answer is no.'

'No what?'

'No, the boss is not in today. Neither is his secretary, Lorraine.'

'Am I allowed to ask when he'll be back?'

'You are, but it won't do you much good. It's sort of like how long is the piece of string.'

'Oh, I see. I had no idea he was going away in the first place, and for an indefinite period, even. Any idea just where our illustrious leader has gone?' Simon asked hopefully.

'Not officially, but Eddie in the accounts department told me he had processed travel claims for the Premier and his secretary for a trip to Tahiti. Eddie said he had a bit of a giggle as the trip, at public expense mind you, is to determine the effects of rising sea levels resulting from global warming. Apparently, a lot of politicians who claim they harbour much the same concerns have made similar study visits to places such as Bolivia, Mongolia and Nepal, all of which seem a little too far away from the ocean to be influenced by any rise in sea level. But no-one ever questions such minor trivialities as it's par for the course. Everyone has their snout in the trough and, provided they can justify their actions are in accordance with the rules, irrespective of how vague an interpretation of those rules might be, no-one questions the ethics or morality of their actions.'

'But how can they justify such expenditure?'

'Aah, come on, sir. Once a politician, the world is their oyster and it can be a bloody big oyster, especially when it's the pollies who set their own rules. Ethics, principles and morality are three words expunged from the politicians' vocabulary once they enter parliament.'

'Boy, Mr Fortesque and his colleagues have really got under your skin. Why don't you quit?' Simon suggested.

'No, I think if I'm able to hang around for a while I'll have enough to write a book on the goings on around here. And if you think Peyton Place was steamy, just you wait and see.'

'Well, I know this place was a bit over the top when it came to the odd bit of philandering, but that was years ago.'

'And nothing's changed. Mr Fortesque does have a wife and family and heaven knows what he tells them when he jaunts off to some exotic, or is that an erotic, place with his secretary. Apart from his dalliance with Lorraine, he seems to have more than his share of regular female visitors.'

'Anyone in particular?'

'Okay, to begin with there's the wife of that politician who just died, Rosetta Blakey. She's been coming in on a fairly regular basis, even before Mr Blakey was done in. And there's this really good-looking lady, Mrs Dawkins. She seems to be a regular.'

'And the nature of their visits?'

Jackie shrugged. 'One can only speculate, but…'

'Heavens to Betsy. You don't mean…?'

'Come on, sir, we all knew what was going on when that politician got himself carved up on Bondi Beach. Nothing's changed, just the people. Look, I'd better get on as there are customers waiting. I'll ring you when the boss gets back and has time to see you.'

Oh, I think the boss will see me whenever I want to see him, Simon thought as he handed Jacky his business card.

⊏⊐

WITH PARKING SPACE AT A PREMIUM, Noel had some distance to walk before his knock on the door of the Chandos Street semi-detached bungalow elicited an unhurried response by a somewhat dishevelled Alf. 'Holy mackerel, don't you blokes ever sleep?' the barefooted, unshaven Alf protested as he took a secure hold of his pyjama pants, an action for which Noel was eternally grateful.

'Sorry, Alf, but it is after nine and I would like to have a chat about the redoubtable Rosetta Stone, if you don't mind?'

'No, not at all. Come on in; I'll put the coffee on.' Without bothering to conceal the exposed upper half of a body that exhibited distinct evidence of prolonged neglect, Alf led Noel down the hallway to the kitchen where, having directed Noel to a chair at the table, he set about making the early morning brew. 'Now, what can I do for you, Serge?'

'Well, she obviously spent some time with you so, as we haven't spoken to her ourselves, we thought you might be able to tell us something about her. You know, did anyone call around to see her; did she make regular telephone calls; what happened to make her want to fleece her husband and then divorce him?'

'Naah, she didn't have any visitors but she went out a few

times, not that I've any idea where she went although she dressed for the city, not the beach, if you know what I mean,' Alf replied as he passed Noel a mug of coffee. 'She was careful with her mobile, always making sure she knew who the caller was before answering, and she wouldn't even go to the loo without it. As far as hubby goes, she did make a few disparaging remarks about him although the one remark she gave most air-time to was when she called him a philandering louse, not that I think she's as virtuous as she would have you believe.'

Noel raised his eyebrows, his curiosity piqued. 'Oh, do tell. What makes you think she's not squeaky clean?'

Alf dragged a chair out from under the table, seated himself and took a sip of coffee. 'As I said, she was surgically attached to her phone. Whenever I heard her talking it seemed to be business like, although there were times when the conversation seemed much more frivolous, women's giggling and cooing sort of thing. Now, I don't know what the gender of the person on the other end was, but Rosetta sounded as silly as a pork chop at times so they weren't talking about the performance of the stock market.'

'So, you think she might have a boy-friend?'

'Or girl-friend. I s'pose it doesn't really matter these days, but it might've given her a good reason to get rid of hubby.'

'Yes, but there are many motives for bumping someone off; jealousy, greed, revenge, hate. We already know that some of these, if not all, apply to Rosetta. Anyway, thanks, Alf. We could sit here and speculate and prognosticate all day, but I have work to do. If you should think of something you might have overlooked, here's my card.' With that, Noel departed leaving the half-naked Alf, still barefooted and stripped to the bottom half of his PJs, to finish off his coffee and contemplate events.

Chapter 12

'Okay, Ron, and what scandals did you dig up on Alvin Stone?' Simon asked as he tapped out a Gene Krupa impersonation with his hands on the armrests of his chair.

'If you take the coroner's report and police records at face value, I'd say there's nothing to suggest Alvin's death was anything but accidental,' Ron said as he scratched the back of his head with one hand and placed the other on his hip. 'He and his wife, Rosetta, were walking around the foreshore path that leads to the mast of *HMAS Sydney* on Bradleys Head. As there's no outrageously high cliffs in the area, Rosetta, according to her statement to police, was not unduly concerned when Alvin left the track and made his way into the bushes, ostensibly to have a pee. When he didn't return, she said she went looking for him only to find him dead at the bottom of a cliffet.'

'Cliffet?' Noel enquired.

'Small cliff,' Ron clarified. 'It seems the police and coroner readily accepted Rosetta's explanation of events. Call me a sceptic, but I think there could be more to Alvin's death than meets the eye.'

'You think Rosetta did him in?' Simon asked, his interest piqued.

Ron shrugged. 'He was a politician so it's not beyond the bounds of possibility. If she did, it would be pretty hard to prove at this late stage even though she probably had motive, means and opportunity. Maybe some discrete enquiries might uncover something new but it's probably not worth the time or effort. And if she did do him in, all that proves is she's capable of murder, and poor Morton might just have been the next in line. Who knows? Maybe Rosetta is waging a personal vendetta against men.'

'Yeah, and you know what they say about the female of the species. Apparently she's been to see the Premier on a few occasions, and the mind boggles as to what the nature of the visits were. Okay, Noel, what are the results of your scrounging around?' Simon asked.

Noel withdrew his notebook from his coat pocket and flicked through the pages until he found what he was looking for. 'According to Alf, Rosetta used her mobile phone rather extensively. Apparently she was always talking to somebody. Of course, he may not be totally familiar with the female propensity to spend hours waffling on to anyone who cares to listen about what knickers she's going to wear for the day, even if it's a wrong number. There was one regular caller who Alf assumed was a female because of the demeanour displayed by Rosetta during the conduct of the conversation. I'm trying to find the identity of whoever this person was through a check of telephone records, which we should get within a day or two.

'As far as B, D and M and the Dawkins go, you'd say everything at first glance was tickety-boo. They've been married for a few years now, Daniel involved in property development at the time of their marriage, and still is, while Jezebel was working in the accounts department up at Parliament House. I took a copy of the marriage certificate,' Noel said and passed it to Ron to pass to Simon; Ron was already standing next to Noel's desk so saved Noel the trouble of unseating himself.

After scrutinising the certificate, Simon looked at Noel and raised his eyebrows. 'So, what am I supposed to be looking at that doesn't make it tickety-boo?'

'The signature of the witness, who was probably the best man,' Noel replied.

Simon opened his desk drawer, took out a magnifying glass and turned on his desk lamp. After spending a couple of minutes of intense study of the document, he turned his light off, replaced his spy glass, sat back and locked his hands behind his head. 'And you think the witness to this nuptial and our current Premier are one and the same person?'

'Yep.'

Ron took up the certificate for his evaluation. 'Yes, and it does have that ring of effrontery about it. Most people sign their name with an initial then the surname. Here our Mr Fortesque wishes it to be known that the signature it's not just that of any Mr Fortesque, but that of Mr Clyde Fortesque. Certainly fits the bill for a politician.'

'Okay,' Simon announced, 'I'm getting a little confused here. We now have a property developer who's a mate of the Premier. We also have the widow of two dead politicians, one positively murdered and one whose death is a little sus to say the least. On top of all that, we still have the outstanding investigation into Robert Porter's stabbing on Bondi Beach.'

Ron, his backside against the two-drawer filing cabinet, squeezed his chin between thumb and forefinger and, after a moment of cogitation, decided to ask, 'And does all this have anything to do with the Taipan Club and Graham Lee?'

After contorting his face into a hideous scowl, Simon relaxed and rested his chin on one hand while he tapped his fingers irritatingly on the desk with the other. Somewhat vexed, he stopped his tapping and responded to Ron's probing question. 'Crikey, Ron, can I take the one on sport instead? How would I know? Something's upsetting Graham and, from what he told me, it has a ring of political involvement. I'm pretty sure it has something to do with the foreign incursion into buying up of real estate assets of which the Taipan Club seems to have been targeted. With the redevelopment of the Taipan site now under question, and with what we've uncovered today, you can bet Morton's death will be involved, somewhere.'

Chapter 13

'So, Graham, what exactly is the position with the sale of the Taipan Club to Glover Property Development?' Simon asked after comfortably settled in Graham Lee's office. 'You've already indicated your intent to sell, or give, the property to GPD for the construction of an apartment block. At the same time, I've heard a rumour Gem Development, or should I say Daniel Dawkins, has taken out an injunction preventing the sale until some problem with the government has been resolved. At least GPD is under the impression the sale will go ahead as I believe they've already submitted conceptual plans to council.' And what's the name of the bloke over there? Henry something or other.'

'Yeah, Henry Haynes who works with Ralph Glover. Ralph took over from the other two Glovers, Paul and cousin Andrew, after the dredged up body from the harbour incident. We all thought, including the attending doctors, that Henry would die following his bashing over at Bondi. Fortunately, he managed to pull through, despite the initial medical claims that he was history.'

'That's right, the Glover twins and that mansion called The Grovel over at Elizabeth Bay,' Simon said with a smile as it was he who had dredged up the body of brother Bruce Glover onto Graham's boat.

Graham Lee, sitting behind his Taipan Club office table, loosened his tie and undid the top button of his shirt. 'Yep, back in the days when things were simple. While the problem I've got at the moment is a bit convoluted, I'm glad you've picked up on of the rumours going around. The truth of the matter is I wanted a residential complex constructed and I needed a developer, GPD, to do it.

'The easiest way through all the red tape, as far as I could see, was for me to donate the site, club and all, to GPD, or sell it for one dollar and let them get on and construct. I'd get a percentage return on my investment with the sale of apartments, as would GPD. The idea was to provide affordable housing to those people who can't afford to scrape up the millions of dollars required as a deposit for some house out the back of Woop Woop. I've already spoken to Henry and he was prepared to develop the place, as long as there was a viable profit margin.

'The problem now is that I don't think I'll have any say in the matter. You're correct in thinking everything with GPD was hunky-dory, that was until this overseas mob, through Gem Development, took legal action and whacked a restraining order to halt proceedings, including the sale of units off the drawing board. I believe the Foreign Investment Review Board is now involved and the State Government intends to take control of any decision on the future of the property. Premier Fortesque has already presented a bill to the house legislating for the approval of the overseas investment, or should I say foreign ownership. This bill was defeated by one vote. They'll try again after someone else is nominated to fill the seat vacated by the death of that bloke, you know, the dissenting voter who went under the train. Irrespective of who it is, he, or she, will soon learn that voting against your own party can be hazardous to your health.'

Simon, lounging in a comfortable lounge chair across the table from Graham, harrumphed and folded his arms. 'So, where does this leave you financially?'

'Fortunately, or unfortunately, I'm a gambling man, not a property developer,' Graham replied. 'I'd say that if the bill gets passed, or when, the place will be sold off to these overseas interlopers at the unimproved property value which will be a zillion dollars short of the market value. Whoever this gate-crasher represents, they'll have so much cash available they could probably buy off Bill Gates. They'll purchase the property at the unimproved value, provide the developer, Gem, with both the capital and the land to construct a you-beaut hotel, and still end up with buckets of money left over.'

'So, if or when the bill gets passed, Gem Development won't have to cough up any money from local investors to build this swanky hotel. Finance for the project will all be provided by the overseas mob which would save the developer a heap of inconvenience by not having to take out bank loans and find financial backers,' Simon muttered. 'So, Graham, you think the polly who wouldn't play ball was done away with because of that very reason?'

'Pounds to doughnuts,' Graham returned. 'Some politician, maybe even the Premier himself, could have set up the hit because of the spanner Morton Blakey threw into the system. The whole deal can't be sanctioned without political support and whoever provides that support will receive a lucrative remuneration for his troubles.'

'And has there been any feedback on GPD's conceptual plans? With the Taipan Club located in Darlinghurst, I believe it falls within the Sydney City Council's bailiwick.'

Graham slowly shook his head. 'No, not a thing which doesn't come as any great surprise. They'll sit on their hands and await an outcome before even going into the zoning aspects of the place which will either be business, as it is now, or high rise residential. I've no doubt someone in the council will receive a nice little bonus from persons unknown once the Premier gets his bill passed and he can satisfy the requirements of this overseas mob. While GPD has submitted their plans to council, you can bet Gem Development is already working on the assumption that the Taipan Club will be transformed into a six-star hotel complex. In fact, I would like to know if any approach has been made to council by Gem.'

'And what do you know about this overseas conglomerate or whatever it is and this David Zheng bloke?' Simon asked.

Graham pursed his lips and gave a shrug. 'Nothing, except they come from China, or Taiwan, or Korea, somewhere over there. The one thing I do know is they've got a lot more money to throw around than I'll ever have, and I don't consider myself down to my last nickel and dime.'

Simon frowned and rubbed his hand across his face. 'Well, I don't know if there's much I can do as far as your problem goes, Graham, but I'm investigating the murder of a politician, probably because he upset the applecart in no short order. I think the time has come for me to have a little talk with Rosetta. I take it she's still on the *Gemini*?

'As far as I know, but I haven't been over there myself for a while. I think Charlie's still working on one of the pumps so there'll be someone home anyway.'

Chapter 14

Both dressed in mufti, including a coat and tie, Detective Chief Inspector Simon Webster and Detective Sergeant Noel Elliott stood out like pimples on a pumpkin as they proceeded along the marina pontoon to where *Gemini* was moored. Generally, most people within the precincts of the marina are dressed in boaty attire; shorts, t-shirt, sneakers and a floppy hat, even in the middle of winter, which it wasn't.

'Anyone home?' Simon called on reaching the fifty-five foot, flybridge luxury cruiser.

'Yes, there is,' came a man's voice from somewhere onboard.

'Well, if that's Charlie Chambers, Noel and I would like to have a chat.'

'Holy hell. Haven't seen you two blokes in yonks now,' said the pale complexion, red haired Charlie as he appeared on the afterdeck, a broad smile on his face.

'No, it seems Graham's a bit too busy to use *Gemini* lately. He's trying to organise the redevelopment of his club. Anyway, permission to come aboard, sir?'

'Of course, by all means. We may as well sit out here as the saloon is undergoing some housework. You're probably on duty, but would you care to splice the mainbrace?' Charlie asked, keeping up the naval idiom.'

'What a good idea,' Noel chimed in before Simon could answer.

Charlie disappeared up the ladder from the afterdeck to the saloon above only to reappear shortly afterwards carrying three cold tinnies. 'Well, gentlemen, I take it you're not here for a social chit-chat.'

Simon wiped away the dripping condensation from the can before he cracked open the tinny and savoured the cold, bitter ale. 'I believe you have a houseguest at the moment?'

'You mean Rosetta Blakey. Yeah, she's just gone up to the shops. Should be back in a tick if you want to speak to her. Nice lady, although I prefer blonds and boaties. I believe she's a friend of Louisa, the boss's wife, although I have no idea what her story is, about being onboard, I mean.'

The conversation was promptly interrupted when a tall brunette dressed in white jeans and a navy blue and pink striped polo top called out from the pontoon. 'Hey, Chick, give us a hand, please? I've a couple of bottles of wine, plus the groceries.'

'Sorry, Rosie,' Charlie replied and, on mounting the gunwale, reached across the small gap between cruiser and pontoon to relieve Rosetta of her load. Once on the afterdeck Charlie turned to Rosetta and introduced her to the two visitors who politely stood for the introductions. 'I'll put these away,' Charlie said, referring to the groceries. 'I'll bring you something to drink, a glass of wine?'

'Love one,' she replied and took a seat. 'Okay, gentlemen, I've an idea what this is about but maybe you'd like to talk about the weather?'

Simon scratched his earlobe, not that it was itchy, and raised his eyebrows. 'No, not really, however there are a couple of things we'd like to get sorted out, the first one being the relationship between you and your husband, or ex-husband.'

Rosetta frowned, the "11" lines between her eyebrows taking on a cavernous appearance before she gave a shrug of inconsequence. 'What's there to tell? I hated the little weasel.'

Noel's whimsical look to Simon conveyed it all – "told you – we have a right proper homicidal maniac here".

Before Simon could pursue the subject, Charley, loaded with three more tinnies and a glass of wine, entered the scene. 'Thought we'd all have anotherie – it's after ten and getting warmer,' he said with a feigned apologetic smile as he handed around the drinks. 'But who needs an excuse?' After gladly accepting the refreshment proffered, Simon continued.

'And Rosetta, you say you hated the little weasel. Could you be a bit more specific and explain the cause of your antipathy towards your little weasel, er, husband?'

'Look, let's get one thing straight from the outset,' Rosetta proclaimed before taking more than a little sip of wine. 'Although I loathed and detested Morton, I didn't kill him. Morton was a politician and I should have known better than to marry him, having worked over in Parliament House myself. I suppose you tend to socialise with those you work with and I admit to socialising rather enthusiastically, even if they all turned out to be a bunch of weasels.'

'You mean a boogle,' Noel broke in.

'A boogle?' Rosetta enquired.

'Yes, a boogle, - bunch of weasels,' Noel clarified.

'Oh. Never heard of it. So, I worked in the middle of a boogle of weasels. How exciting.'

'And was Alvin Stone a weasel too?' Simon enquired with the expressed purpose of asking the unexpected.

Rosetta's eyes widened, obviously struck by the relevance of Simon's enquiry. 'And what's Alvin Stone got to do with this mess? He stuffed up his life over ten years ago.'

'No, no, no, Rosetta. We're asking the questions. Now, did you happen to consider Alvin Stone a weasel?'

Rosetta gave another frown. 'DCI Webster, the simple

answer to your question is an emphatic yes, and the answer to your next question is a just as emphatic; no, I didn't push Alvin over the cliff, but I might have had I'd thought of it. If I was going to murder anyone during those days it would probably have been Robert Porter, the lecherous degenerate.'

Noel, always interested in a bit of scandal which would later, no doubt, be the subject of a discussion by those sitting on Simon's back lawn and sipping a quiet refreshment, couldn't refrain from asking, 'Now, what in the world would your reason be to want to do that, Rosetta? After all, it seems you weren't the only person wanting to bump off Mr Porter.'

'Charlie, could I have another one of these, please?' Rosetta asked as she handed Charlie her empty glass before turning her attention back to Noel. 'DS Elliott, around that time Robert and I were what you might call an item, despite me being a married woman. Well, I thought we were an item as we seemed to spend a lot of time up at The Hydro in The Blue Mountains. Anyway, damned if he didn't give me the flick and went off to marry Louisa, poor girl. It came as a complete surprise, at least to me. It seemed everyone else in the place knew what was going on so I ended up looking like a real pea-brain. I know, I know, history repeats itself and I should have known better.'

'Meaning?' Noel asked.

Rosetta harrumphed. 'Robert Porter had had a tryst with Monica Sainsbury before we got together so I s'pose he dumped her to take up with me. Maybe that's one of the reasons why she bumped him off.'

A surprised look came over the face of both detectives. 'You don't mean the Monica Sainsbury who married Wally Ackerman, the Deputy Premier?' Simon asked, somewhat perplexed.

'Yes, the one and only dear, sweet, wouldn't hurt a fly, Monica. And if you believe that, you're nuts. She was hard as nails and couldn't tolerate fools, which is a sort of a contradiction in terms seeing she married a politician. She ran a construction or development business in the eastern suburbs and we'd see her around the Premier's office fairly regularly. I have no doubt such visits were to provide her the opportunity to cultivate political support for whatever she might need political support for, usually some redevelopment scam. I hear tell Porter, as a government MP, upped his price for his support in the awarding of government contracts which may have furthered her inclination to do away with the imbecile.'

Simon turned to Noel, the expression on his face conveying a million words. 'See, it had to be Monica,' Simon said with gratification. 'All we have to do now is fish her out of the Amazon and charge her with murder.' With his mind initially on the Blakey murder, Rosetta's unexpected disclosure to the two detectives proved too much for Simon who couldn't help but be side-tracked to the Porter murder. 'So, who else believes Monica is the guilty party?' Simon asked.

'Oh, would you believe everyone? At least, all the girls around parliament knew, with the possible exception of Louisa,' Rosetta replied. 'It took Louisa a lot of time and a marriage to Porter for her to realise he was just using her as a good-looking accoutrement to be dragged along to social functions. No-one told Louisa of Porter's debauchery and his flings with other women, that was her problem. Anyway, one thing led to another and when Monica said she could kill Porter, we all thought she was joking. When we learnt that she was serious, neither Jezebel, with whom I worked with up in Parliament House, nor myself were going to do anything to discourage Monica of her plan to do away with Porter. In fact, we would have been happy to draw straws for the job. It's just that Monica got in first and hacked him up on Bondi Beach. But I thought you'd know all about that?'

'Yes, well, we didn't get the opportunity to speak to Monica before she shot off to Brazil, although we always had the idea she was probably the guilty party. And did Wally know what was going on?' Noel asked.

'Probably not. Wally might have been the deputy Premier but I don't think he knew what day of the week it was. In fact, I think the poor bloke blew a diode in his circuitry and the mother-ship abandoned him,' Rosetta responded with a smirk on her face.

Now, conscious of the fact that the little chat with Rosetta wasn't going to be a five-minute job, Simon removed his coat and draped it over the back of his chair. 'Okay Rosetta, although we'll need to have a bit of a chat about Mr Porter's death, we are looking into the murder of another politician. Now, what's the story with you and Morton?'

Rosetta gladly accepted Charlie's offered refreshment of the bottle of Chardonnay before replying. 'Morton was supposed to be a high flyer in politics and I thought it might be fun to hitch my wagon and go along for the ride. It never mattered to us girls whether our target was married or not, in fact it was preferable they were. He was a backbencher when I met him, sometime after Alvin's death, oh, I suppose at least ten or so years ago. After we were married, he was promoted to a position within the ministry which didn't last long before the Premier recognised his capabilities, or lack thereof, and shunted him back to the backbenches.

'It was around then that he went really strange, you know, nuts is probably a better diagnosis. Everything he did had to be rationalize altruistically, including every bill introduced into parliament. If he didn't agree, to hell with party lines, he'd do as he pleased and vote accordingly. I doubt if the party would've endorsed him for the next election as he was more of an Independent. Here Morton was with both feet on the gravy train with boundless opportunity to make more money than you could poke a stick at and he adopts a holier than thou attitude.

'Anyway, the star I thought I had hitched my wagon to

turned out to be the *Titanic*. The marriage was headed for disaster and it was time I started to take steps to abandon ship.'

'And you thought you might give Morton the flick after squeezing as much money out of him as you could before you spent your hard-earned cash on a solicitor?' Noel enquired.

'Far better to spend his money on a divorce than mine, and that's where the kidnapping idea came in. And DCI Webster, for the third time today, no, I didn't kill Morton nor have I killed anybody else for that matter.'

A silence enveloped the group as Simon and Noel considered their situation. In an effort to maintain some momentum, Noel looked at Rosetta questionably. 'As you haven't knocked off anyone, why are you hiding away over here and not living back at home? It's not as though Morton is waiting on the doorstep to do you mischief.'

Rosetta slowly shook her head. 'Well, if he is, we're all in deep trouble. But DS Elliott, I may have been the wife of a lowly backbencher, but I was the wife of a lowly backbencher who happened to get himself assassinated. While you may think the murder of a politician is an everyday event, there are those who may think otherwise. Unfortunately, the paparazzi is capable of making a mountain out of a molehill and could sensationalize a sloth climbing up a tree. If I returned home now, I would have had to run the gauntlet of a rampant mob of camera swinging flee-brained reporters. In a day or two Morton's death will be past history and no-one will give a stuff about whatever happened yesterday.'

'Crikey, sorry I asked,' returned Noel, suitably rebuked. 'But one question we need to ask, where were you on the day Morton collided with the train?'

'I was here trying to get some peace and quiet,' Rosetta replied with more than a touch of exasperation. 'After bird-brain Benny had virtually sent the police an invitation regarding the kidnapping, I wasn't going to hang around at Alf's place and wait for a SWAT team to arrive.'

'And is there anyone who can confirm that?' Simon asked.

'What? That I didn't want to wait around for the police to arrive?'

'No, that you were here.' Simon refrained from adding a caustic comment that may have exacerbated a situation already becoming a trifle unpleasant.

Rosetta turned to Charlie and said, more as a statement than anything else, 'Charlie, you can vouch for me.'

Charlie's bottom lip dropped and he slowly nodded. 'Yeah, we were here until lunchtime then I had to race off to a chandler over at Drummoyne. I didn't get back until after seven.'

Again, Simon decided against stoking the embers and, with eyebrows raised, gave Rosetta a wry look which, in turn, elicited nothing more than a look of cynical indifference.

As the mood on the afterdeck was taking on one of unsociable irritation and annoyance, Charley, whose presence was not mandatory, if not intrusive from the outset, excused himself and retired to the fly bridge as far away from the afterdeck as possible. Charlie liked Rosetta regardless of the fact that he had detected a streak of malice bubbling away just below the surface of propriety and respectability. But there again, Rosetta had to display some degree of decorum, at least while Morton held a seat in parliament, but Morton was now dead.

'So, Rosetta, who do you think planted the knife in your husband's back and shoved him out in front of a train just to make sure he was dead?' Simon asked, all pretence of civility brushed aside.

Rosetta pressed her lips together and pondered the question for a few moments. 'DCI Webster, Morton had the opportunity to make a lot of money, quite apart from the scams and financial remuneration payable for nothing more than a nod of assent in the House. Unfortunately, Morton and his newfound altruistic perspective on life put him offside with many of his colleagues, including the Premier who must be shedding crocodile tears over his death. Naturally, in view of the nature of Morton's departure from politics, his place in government will be taken by a member of the same party, an event I'm sure the Premier is anxiously awaiting.'

'You think the Premier might have done him in?' Noel asked.

'I'm sorry, DS Elliott, but I haven't a clue as to who "did him in" as you so politely put it and, to be honest, I really don't give a damn who did him in. The important thing is that some kind-hearted person did. My first priority now is for me to visit my solicitor and find out how much the little weasel has left me, and it better be heaps or I'll dig him up and stick a knife into him just for the satisfaction of making sure he is dead.'

Simon looked a trifle concerned, the fingers on his right hand subconsciously tapping out a rhythm on the chair's armrest. In an effort to establish the financial damage caused by Morton's floor-crossing exercise, Simon asked, 'You said Morton could have made a lot of money for nothing more than a nod of the head. Are you saying he may have jeopardised the opportunity for some of his colleagues to profit financially by his unfavourable response to a particular bill in parliament?'

Rosetta shrugged. 'I have no idea, but I do know there's a certain property developer who stands to make millions on a recent redevelopment scheme. There's some glitch which has prompted government intervention into the proposal although I have no idea the ins and outs of what was going, something to do with overseas ownership or investment.'

'Any idea of the property in question?' Noel queried.

'The Taipan Club,' came Rosetta's lucid reply.

Chapter 15

'Getting right off the Taipan problem for a moment and turning to the personal issues, Rosetta, what do you know about Jezebel Dawkins and her husband, who is it? Oh yes, Daniel, Daniel Dawkins.'

Rosetta's countenance brightened appreciably, the subject of Jezebel Dawkins apparently far more appealing than whatever might happen to the Taipan Club or whoever the murderer of her husband might be. 'Oh, I've known Jezebel for years. We started off together as junior clerks in Parliament House a million years ago. Okay, not quite a million, but it seems like a lot of water has passed under the bridge since then. What is it exactly that you want to know?'

Noel rocked back on his chair, his arms folded. 'First off, we believe Jezebel was Morton's campaign manager?' he asked, his statement posed with a questioning look.

Rosetta nodded. 'Yes, that's right, and "was" is the operative word. I very much doubt if she'd give Morton the time of day now, if he was still alive, that is.'

'Oh, and why's that?' Noel queried.

Before answering, Rosetta ran her fingers through her long dark hair, the expression on her face one of contemplative reflection as she decided how best to answer. After a brief pause, she sat back and steepled her fingers. 'As I said before, Jezebel and I have been good mates, well, mates anyway, for a long time and have shared quite a few experiences. I don't deny that during our days working at Parliament House things got pretty wild.'

'Pretty wild?' Noel, seeking some elaboration on just what Rosetta meant by "pretty wild", asked.

'Well, I suppose wild is subjective,' Rosetta returned with a smile. 'You see, most of the men there were out in the big wide world, away from their mummy and daddy or spouses for the first time in their life. There were three of us, Jezebel, Louisa and myself, and we'd see who could latch on to the politician offering the biggest scam. Most of the scams involved trips interstate which might have been labelled, euphemistically, as dirty weekends but weren't as they happened during the week to make everything look kosher. Sure, we knew there was a price to be paid but after a few glasses of wine, who cared.

'Unfortunately, I should have known better and not let emotions get in the way of a good time, which is what happened when I picked up Alvin, who was single at the time. Champagne and caviar, five-star hotels, and all on the tax payer funded expense account. What else could a girl ask for?' Anyway, to cut a long story short, we finally decided to get married. However, after a couple of years Alvin ran up the true colours of the politician and that was the end of any matrimonial harmony that may have existed. Fortunately for me Alvin decided to jump off a cliff and do himself some terminal damage. I have no idea why he did it although I did hear a rumour one of the secretaries was taking out a paternity suit against him. I dare say that might have caused him just a little angst. And yes, I know the police had the idea I may have pushed him over. The silly thing is, if I wanted to do away with him by shoving him over a cliff, I wouldn't have chosen one where there was a distinct possibility he would survive. As you're probably aware, the cliffs around Bradleys Head aren't the highest in the city precincts.'

'Yeah okay, but you can break your neck getting out of the bathtub, more's the pity. I take it Louisa took up with Robert Porter and had the same thing happen to her, marriage failure I mean?' Noel speculated

'Look, DS Elliott,' Rosetta said dryly, 'I could hardly tell Louisa she was doing the wrong thing, but the fact of the matter is, as I have already told you, Robert Porter and I had been an item at one stage. Robert and Alvin had been friends with the same predisposition for frequent philandering and both Louisa and I were remarkedly stupid, although at different times. Porter gave me the old heave-ho to take up with Louisa although I know he and the wife of the Minister for Sport, Cheryl, Cheryl Mason, had a thing going for a while. I seem to remember that was before he took up with Louisa. Fortunately for everyone concerned, someone ended up hating him more than either Louisa or myself and that someone was Monica Ackerman. She certainly has my admiration, wherever she is, as she stitched him up quite effectively, and on Bondi Beach too.'

'And the marriage of Jezebel and Daniel Dawkins of Gem Property Development. Everything hunky-dory there?' Simon asked.

'Jezebel married Daniel while she was working up in Parliament House and he was making a mint out of government contracts, which he was receiving on a regular basis, and still is. The funny thing is he never seems to have to tender for a contract. Daniel and Clyde Fortesque have been friends since school days, not that that should make any difference, but I'm sure it does,' Rosetta explained.

'Yes, but my question sought your opinion as to whether Jezebel and Daniel were happily married, not the relationship between Daniel and the Premier'.

Rosetta harrumphed. 'Well, it might've been at first as she didn't marry some weasel. Although she left parliament and joined Daniel and the development company, she maintained her friendship with those she used to work with. She became Morton's campaign manager for the last election as she had experience with politicians, was aware of election campaign strategy and had a fair idea of what the job entailed. Apparently the job description included some nebulous clause in the small print requiring the successful applicant to sleep with him which, for Jezebel, wouldn't have been anything unusual.'

'You mean Jezebel was sleeping with Morton?' Noel asked, somewhat vexed by the revelation.

'Course she was.'

'And neither you nor Daniel minded,' Noel pursued.

'Not in the least, well, at least I didn't, and I'm sure Daniel didn't. Later, after the affair, Jezebel told me Morton had said he planned to leave me and marry her, which is par for the course for a married man. She claimed she was never emotionally involved with Morton. However, as there were definite cracks in her relationship with Daniel, she set about a more independent lifestyle.'

'Which included a bit of hanky-panky. However, you still haven't answered my question as to the recent animosity between Jezebel and Morton,' Noel reminded Rosetta.

'Well, I believe the thing that took a real beating was her pride when she realised Morton had no inclination whatsoever to divorce me. That really upset her, which surprised me as she had told me she wasn't emotionally involved. Maybe she was. I could have told her Morton would never leave me as he needed me to at least give the impression he was a happily married man, and a trustworthy person to represent their electorate in parliament. And once he'd won his seat, Morton gave her the old heave-ho, which wasn't too polite of him. Ho-hum.'

Simon looked at Noel who, after ceasing his notetaking in

the notebook taken from his coat pocket, returned Simon's gaze with a look of bemusement and a shrug of the shoulders. 'Getting back to the two, maybe three murders,' Simon continued, 'in effect, the three of you, Louisa, Jezebel and yourself, had motive for doing a dastardly deed on the respective politician each of you were involved with? I've included Louisa while recognising your comments relating to Monica Sainsbury and Robert Porter.'

Rosetta refrained from an immediate comment, her first priority being a recharge of her glass with the dregs of the Chardonnay. 'DCI Webster, if you believe we all had a motive, it was certainly not of our making. The politicians involved were all just playing the same game all politicians play; rorting the gravy train, scamming the system, and looking for a bit on the side. If we had a motive for moving one or two members of the boogle off the planet, it's only because they provided us with the motive, and on a silver platter to boot.'

'Just one last question, Rosetta. I believe both you and Jezebel made regular trips to see Premier Fortesque. Can you tell me the nature of such visits?' Simon asked.

Rosetta pursed her lips and frowned before taking a deep breath in resignation. 'I've never liked Clyde Fortesque but I liked my husband even less. To put it bluntly, I was providing the Premier with any indication of Morton's way of thinking on up-coming bills so he might be able to circumvent the possibility of a vote of no confidence. The government was, is, on very shaky ground with a one seat majority and the last thing the Premier needs is a loose cannon sitting in the back-benches.

'As far as Jezebel's visits go, I can only assume the awarding of government contracts to Gem Development without the tender requirement comes at a cost. Maybe Jezebel's visits are made so she can take the opportunity to suitably reimburse the Premier for his consideration. Maybe that's being a bit harsh as I really have no idea as to the nature of her visits as we never called on the Premier at the same time. Anyway, it's not like Jezebel would balk at the price she had to pay, or is paying, if the cost is what I think it might be, but don't quote me. I think there isn't much Jez wouldn't do to ensure the ongoing benefits her husband is reaping. After all, it's just a case of whatever belongs to Daniel belongs to Jezebel.'

Before disembarking from the good ship *Gemini*, Simon turned to Rosetta. 'Just one last thing, Rosetta, do you have anyone lined up for husband number three now Morton's dead?'

'Oh yes. But that's confidential and I choose not to discuss the matter.'

Simon looked at Noel and slowly shook his head. Holy hell, what a mess, Simon thought. I wonder if Daniel is aware Rosetta has him lined up for her next marital victim.

Chapter 16

Noel meticulously folded the sheet of paper into something resembling the shape of a streamlined aircraft. After a close inspection of his handiwork, and holding great expectations, he launched the aircraft in the direction of where Simon was currently sitting at the far end of the office. Needless to say, the exercise only proved beyond doubt that Noel's ability in aircraft design and construction was matched only by his ability in basketball shooting.

'Okay, boss, what's on the agenda now?' Noel asked as he picked up his pen and started to subconsciously click the nib annoyingly, as was his bent. 'Although all the women currently involved had a motive for killing someone or other, we're not investigating someone or other's murder; it's Morton Blakey's murderer we're after.'

Simon closed his eyes and squeezed the bridge of his nose as he pondered Noel's profound, if not pithy comment. After a moment he sat back and scratched a non-itchy earlobe. 'In light of what we've learnt from the Premier and Graham Lee, there's every possibility the death of Mr Blakey may not be attributable to the fairer sex. I'm beginning to get the feeling Blakey's murder and his holier than thou attitude displayed in parliament may have a connection with the sale of the Taipan Club. Obviously his dissent on the overseas ownership issue cost a few people a bundle of money. On top of that, I think Blakey might have got up the nose of Daniel Dawkins to the extent that even he might have given Blakey the old heave-ho. In the meantime, I want you to go over to Immigration and see what they have on a Mister David Zheng. You know, who he is, date of arrival in country, previous visits, etcetera.

'And who, might I ask, is David Zheng when he's home?' Noel asked, rather surprised at the mention of the unfamiliar name.

'That, my dear Watson, is what you're to trundle off to Immigration to find out. It seems he's been a regular visitor to the Premier's office lately. Following overtures from Zheng, the Premier is now trying to push through a bill in parliament for overseas ownership of property in the heart of Sydney. With Blakey having done his best to thwart the vote, I'm not discounting the possibility Mr Zheng might be involved in his death. Once you find out a bit more info, we'll do a character check on him through authorities in whatever country he hails from.'

Noel harrumphed. 'Well, I guess whatever his character is, we can discount any involvement with the Cosa Nostra as his name doesn't seem to fit the bill for that mob. I take it you believe he's involved with the purchase of the Taipan Club?'

'I'm certain of it as the Premier has confirmed Zheng's involvement, that's if the Premier isn't telling us untruths. It seems politicians would rather adopt a head in the sand approach to overseas buyers currently targeting our property like the Oklahoma '93 land rush. We just didn't hear the cannon go off.'

'Okay, boss, I'll get right on to it,' Noel said as he, in a brief display of energetic animation, bounced out of his chair and headed for the door.

Simon leant back on his chair and, in a reflective mood,

drummed his fingers on the table. Whether he liked it or not, he knew he was being inexorably drawn into the unscrupulous world of the politician. It was probably by sheer coincidence that as he had that rather noxious thought, he received a phone call from Jackie. The Premier had returned.

━━━

'PREMIER FORTESQUE, I presume you are aware that I'm currently investigating the death of Morton Blakey, so tragically murdered recently in the heart of the city. I believe his death came not long after he crossed the floor of the House to vote with the opposition against a bill introduced by yourself for the approval of foreign ownership, as opposed to foreign investment, of a city property and, ultimately, the construction of a six-star hotel complex.'

'Well first off, DCI Webster, I can confirm your presumption. Someone's dead and I'd expect the police to be investigating, even if the victim was a member of the backbenches. While Morton Blakey voted against the bill, the only outcome he achieved was to delay the inevitable. We'll get it passed, one way or the other in the not too distant future. The second point I wish to make is the significance you place on the time factor of his death. As such significance might be construed as being somewhat suggestive, I take it you believe his murder was bound up with his little display of petulance?'

'And there, Mr Premier, you have hit the nail on the head and the reason for my visit. I have no beliefs, only baseless suppositions, hearsay and one or two confirmed facts at this stage. While I have no axe to grind with any particular politician of any political persuasion, the fact is Mr Blakey must have been aware that his decision to cross the floor was going to prove an embarrassment for the government and a career limiting move on his part. As he was a member of your government, you must have some idea as to what prompted his decision to cross the floor?'

The Premier pouted before he pushed his chair back from his ego bolstering table and slowly shook his head. 'DCI Webster, I have absolutely no idea, although you could speculate all day. He was more of an Independent than a party team player and lately he had come up with all these stupid and absurd public-spirited ideas.'

'That would suggest he believed the bill wasn't kosher,' Simon said with a questionable look.

'Maybe he just wanted to be a nark,' the Premier replied. 'After all, it was my bill and I introduced it.'

'You mean Morton was waging a personal vendetta against you?'

'As I said, you can speculate all you want.'

Simon settled back in the leather lounge chair and extracted a notebook from his coat pocket. 'By your own admission, Mr Premier, I believe all this kafuffle relates back to a property currently owned by a Mr Graham Lee and occupied as the Taipan Club. Mr Lee currently has plans for the property which involves the construction of a residential complex. Now, following certain meetings between yourself and an Asian businessman, whom you have identified as Mr Zheng, an injunction has been taken out by Gem Development against Mr Lee preventing him from proceeding with his plans. While it may be sheer coincidence, the person who actually took out the injunction, Daniel Dawkins, just happens to be in collusion with Mr Zheng. Together they're pushing their own plans for a six-star hotel to be built on the property. As far as Graham Lee is concerned, the manner in which this overseas interest is acting is nothing short of hostile. Obviously, individuals acting for the cartel are seeking political support which you have provided by introducing a bill permitting foreign ownership of a piece of land in the middle of the city.'

The Premier, his arms still folded, started to gently rock back and forward on his chair. 'My, my, if I think about that, I'm sure I would find some scurrilous accusations being thrown around. But, as we are in private with no witnesses, the answer is yes, Mr Zheng has approached me on a number of occasions seeking my support and, I admit, he prompted my bill to parliament. But as I said, Blakey only deferred the end result as the government can acquire land if it so chooses.

'It comes down to whether Mr Zheng pays Mr Lee for the property, or we, the government, acquires the land and sells it on to Mr Zheng. The difference here is that if Mr Lee was to sell the property on the open market to Mr Zheng, or anybody else for that matter, he would ask the market price whereas we have the muscle to take possession of the Taipan Club and on-sell it to Zheng at a much lower price. Naturally Mr Lee will receive compensation from the government for the take-over of the property, although I expect that amount will be far less than what he might expect. It is unfortunate that things haven't gone exactly as planned and we can put that down to Mr Blakey's performance. Both Mr Zheng and I have been quite irritated by events as we expected everything to be squared away by now.'

'But government can only acquire privately held land if it's for public purposes,' Simon declared, a little annoyed that the prospects of his friend's proposed residential redevelopment scheme seemed headed for oblivion.

'And a six-star hotel wouldn't be for public purposes?'

Simon refrained from answering but gave a conceding shrug and a nod. 'And you don't see any illegality in your involvement, like a conflict of interest?'

'None whatsoever, despite the innuendo. Any action I have taken to assist our overseas friend, Mr Zheng, has been totally within the guidelines and any action or processes currently in train are perfectly legal.'

Chapter 17

Despite the forecast of a southerly change later in the day, Simon had prepared the back lawn for an afternoon of congenial company and maybe the odd one or two light ambers, or wine depending on preference. To Simon's mind the weather bureau man, who obviously hadn't taken the time to look outside the window to view the current utopian conditions, had based his calamitous afternoon forecast of hurricanes, tornadoes and the coming of the second deluge on nothing more than what is euphemistically referred to as a SWAG or, to be a tad less dignified, a scientific wild arse guess.

With the morning sun shining brightly and not a cloud in the sky, a solitary beady-eyed seagull had already perched itself on the nearby fence, fully conscious of the fact that the round table placed on the lawn would soon be stocked with beak watering nibblies. While not quite the sea-going fare of seagulls, such readily available sustenance was thought, at least by this seagull, to be significantly more convenient than having to fly all over the stupid wet, waterlogged ocean seeking a cold and unappetizing fishy thing to satisfy the pangs of a gull's hunger.

The early preparation for the afternoon's get-together had

been prompted by Simon's growing expectancy that something was definitely rotten in the state of wherever. His little discussion with the Premier had done nothing to allay his growing concern that the Premier himself might not be as kosher as he would have you believe. Along with the arrival of the expected guests that included the Lees, Elliotts, Ron and Judy, came the opportunity to discuss the two aspects of Morton Blakey's murder Simon considered somewhat intriguing; the nefarious political involvement in the attempted overseas takeover of the Taipan Club property, and the most basic of all motives to murder someone, the jilted wife or lover.

———

'SO, Louisa, you say that everything Rosetta told us is basically true?' Simon asked after having provided the details of the *Gemini* discussion.

Louisa subconsciously laid a placating hand on Graham's arm. 'Yes, although viewed from Rosetta's point of view, naturally. Either one way or the other, we all had a motive for killing off a politician or two. I could have killed Porter while Rosetta had 'em lined up with Alvin, Morton and Porter all candidates for the chop. And don't forget dear old Jezebel who had good reason to eliminate Morton and probably wouldn't shed a tear if Daniel got hit by a bus. It's odd, isn't it? All of us with motive and not a murderer to be found.'

'And Graham, you knew what was going on?' Simon enquired as he rocked back and forth on his director chair.

Graham finished pouring a glass of Chardonnay before he answered. 'My knowledge is limited to events after Louisa left Robert Porter and before he was murdered. In fact, I don't think there's anything of significant importance in Louisa's background that I am unaware of. Yes, I could possibly have arranged for someone to do the hit on Robert, but the situation never arose as Louisa and I were happy to let the sands of time pass unsullied which, as things turned out, happened to be the perfect decision.'

Simon tossed his empty tinny into the metal garbage bin with a clunk and reached for another from the esky beside his chair. 'Okay, Ron, have you come up with anything?'

'Well, I took a look at the relationship between Fortesque and Dawkins as there does appear to be some close association there, especially in view of the marriage certificate. It seems they both went to Grammar at the same time and were good buddies. Fortesque has always had money although it's rumoured Dawkins bankrolled his election campaign. And let's face it, no politician would ever dream of pouring his own money into financing his own re-election campaign when he can spend someone else's, and we know what the quid pro quo was, or is, for Dawkins. Fortesque's married, although that doesn't prevent him from the occasional fling, and it's said Madam Fortesque tries to hold the purse strings in their marriage while he tends to spend it. Apart from that, that's it.'

Of the four women present, it was Louisa, somewhat miffed at the direction the conversation had taken, turned an irate look upon Simon. 'Look, Simon, the discussion has gone off the rails. Here we were talking about the involvement of a number of women in a gruesome murder case and as soon as you men get involved, it's about men and politics and nothing to do with murder.'

'And what, pray I, gives you the idea politicians and developers can't indulge in a little homicide whenever they might have the inclination?' Noel interjected. 'Morton Blakey's murder, as far as we can tell, was predicated on either women's personal involvement and their relationship with Blakey, or on the fact that he screwed the Premier's bill preventing the overseas purchase of the Taipan Club, at least for the moment. At this juncture you can toss a coin because I believe both sides have the propensity and motive for murder.'

'And I for one support Louisa's take on the situation,' Judy responded. 'Even in our little circle here we have Georgie who wasn't backward in taking Dorothy out of play for no other reason than her dislike for the woman.'

'Hey, hang on a sec,' interposed Georgie. 'I haven't a malevolent bone in my body. Dorothy's death was an accident and in no way did I contribute to her death.'

Louisa closed her eyes and slowly shook her head. 'Sorry, Georgie, I didn't mean to spark a row. I was only trying to make the point that the female is just as deadly as the male, which only confirms what Mr Kipling had to say. I admit, if the opportunity had presented itself, I would've been very happy to shuffle Robert Porter off the planet. Obviously there was someone with a similar loathing I had for the man and, fortunate for me, whoever that person was had the nerve to eradicate the cretin. After that, Graham here took me under his wing for which I will be eternally grateful.'

Graham looked at Louisa and gave a subtle wink before refilling her glass with Chardonnay. 'Yes, thanks, sweetie. I think I'll need a few of these,' Louisa said. ''Tis a nice drop and very moreish.'

'Don't think so, Louisa,' Noel butted in, 'this Chard's made in Australia and I don't think the Moors were making it, at least not while they were in Spain or Portugal.' As a conversation stopper, Noel was unsurpassed and he had, again, excelled himself with some trivial but illuminating aspects of the wine industry, for which no-body seemed the least bit interested, especially Louisa.

'Aah Louisa, maybe I've forgotten to mention it, but the rumour has it your dearly departed and loving ex-husband was stabbed to death by Monica Sainsbury, you know, the girl married to Wally Ackerman,' Simon's announcement breaking the embarrassing silence but causing nothing more than a ripple of surprise from the four women present.

'Well, that surprises me like a petrol price rise at Christmas time,' came Louisa's caustic response. 'Porter dumped Monica quicker than a hot potato, not that I'm aware of the specific reason, but something upset her rather severely. She was paying Porter for government contracts and maybe something went wrong. Anyway, it wasn't too long after Monica's break-up that Porter and I had a bit of a fling and ended up tying the knot. Bad mistake; it ended in a disastrous marriage.'

'So, Louisa, as you are one of the three, and I'm not refer-ring to the three witches in that play, do you believe you all had it within yourselves to commit murder?' Simon asked.

'What, you mean Jezebel, Rosetta and myself? Hell, yes. Look, there's one thing men will never understand. Although women come from Venus and men from Mars, we can be just as ruthless and cut-throat as men, the difference being women tend to try to be a bit more subtle about it. Rosetta might well have murdered two husbands, and both Jezebel and I had good reason to murder Porter, while Jezebel could have done Blakey in, I suppose. And I wouldn't mind betting your rumour-monger is right and Monica did carve up Mr Porter, bless her little heart. The thing you have to decide is whether Blakey was murdered by a woman or a man, for entirely different reasons.'

Chapter 18

'So, Louisa thinks women can be more subtle than men when it comes to a merciless massacre. I can't help thinking Louisa would be as subtle as a bloody train wreck if provoked,' Noel said as he reflected back on the weekend's discussions on Simon's back lawn. 'But she's absolutely right; Blakey was murdered by either a man, a woman or someone who can't decide.'

Simon threw his pen onto his desk, sat back and rubbed his eyes with the balls of his hands. After mulling over Noel's comment, he folded his arms and gazed at Noel with a sense of wonder. 'You know, Noel, if Fisher ever asks you how the investigation's going, I suggest you keep your thoughts to yourself. I'm fully aware that there are three genders nowadays, but we generally refer to only males and females so I'm almost certain the guilty person must be one or the other.

'At the moment I'm inclined to think the women have the edge on motive. Sure, Blakey might have upset the applecart and put a few noses out of joint. Problem is there's such a proliferation of similar political scams being perpetrated involving foreign ownership. And there's the rub. With foreign investment we gain a financial benefit whereas with foreign ownership we get no economic benefit, it all goes into the coffers of the country concerned. And if we plebs can identify the difference between ownership and investment, why can't the politicians who are selling off the country as if there's no tomorrow, unless it's in their personal financial interest to do so. And that's where Mr Blakey demonstrated his altruistic nature by voting against the Foreign Ownership Bill which only went to prove that you can get yourself killed for voting against your own party.'

'So, at this stage you're not discounting the possibility some disgruntled polly whacked him?' Noel suggested, wishing to contribute something meaningful to the conversation after his admonishment.

'I'm not discounting anything. All I'm saying is that we have three women, all with motive and, according to Louisa, all with the intestinal fortitude to commit murder. We'll need to interview the ladies, especially to determine the opportunity angle. Oh, by the way, did you come up with anything on our Mr Zheng?'

Noel rummaged through his "In" basket and withdrew a single sheet of handwritten paper. 'Yeah, not much at the moment. He's a Chinese national and has been to Australia on a few occasions, ostensibly to look over real estate. Immigration has no reason not to issue him with a visa, and that applies to his travelling companion, a Mr John Chang, who travels with Mr Zheng on a regular basis. I've asked the police in Hong Kong if they know of him, or his companion, and am awaiting a response, which may take some time, if ever.'

'And what makes you think his apparent real estate interest is not what it seems?' Simon asked.

Noel scratched behind his ear as he decided just how he should couch his response, not having anything to support his gut feeling. 'First off, I don't want you to get the idea I'm xenophobic or anything like that, but there's an awful lot of real estate being bought up by overseas buyers loaded with buckets of money; a million here, a million there. To my mind, that's all small bikkies for the likes of Mr Zheng. I think he's here for undisclosed purposes and you can speculate all you like as to what those purposes might be.'

'So, he wants to build a hotel which seems okay to me. The problem is that the chances of Graham getting a fair price for the club seem pretty remote, what with the Premier's support of Mr Zheng,' Simon responded.

'Well, I still smell a rat as a hotel would just provide Zheng a legitimate facility to further whatever illicit activity he may wish to pursue here in Australia.'

'Aah, come on. We don't know anything about Mr Zheng. There's nothing to suggest he's a criminal and I'm sure the Premier has made discrete inquiries about the gentleman.'

Noel pressed his lips together and gave an acknowledging shrug. 'Okay, but I still reckon something stinks.'

<hr />

'GOOD GRIEF, I haven't seen you blokes in ages,' the tall, brown eyed female barista commented as Simon, Noel and Ron entered the coffee shop on the corner of George and Bathurst Streets. 'Two flat blacks and a cappuccino?'

'Good memory, Flitch,' Noel replied with a smile. Flitch was, in reality, Felicity but everyone who knew Felicity called her Flitch.

After settling into a window seat to await their morning brew, it was Simon who initiated the discussion. 'It's unfortunate, but I have this idea an interview with the Premier may be a total waste of time for no other reason than he's in dire need of a reality check. But then again, he might just be living in a state of total ignorance, which is probably more to the point.'

'Well, I wouldn't put my money on it,' Ron remarked.

'Zheng has bigger fish to fry than just building a hotel and all the Premier can see is what Zheng wants him to see.'

At that moment, Flitch arrived with the three cups of coffee which were duly distributed with an engaging smile. 'Been a while, so let's not leave it so long until next time,' Flitch rebuked the group of men with feigned indignation.

'I'm inclined to agree with Noel's assessment of the situation,' Ron continued 'meaning any development by Zheng, be it hotel, shopping centre or whatever, would be just a front for the real business at hand.'

'And what might that be, money laundering?' Simon mused.

Ron indicated his "could be" response by a spreading the hands, palms up, a nod of the head, a purse of the lips and a "haven't a clue" shrug.

'And you think our illustrious Premier doesn't want to know, just as long as he gets his three thousand ducats from Mr Zheng, if or when he gets his bill passed?' Simon asked as he harked back to Noel's train of thought.

Ron harrumphed. 'Fortesque ain't no Venetian merchant, but he is a politician and will grab whatever he can while he can. Politicians, not having the nous to know the difference between right and wrong, have this knack of saying "I've done nothing wrong" when referring to their actions, legal or illegal, and to hell with the moral or ethical issues. I suppose that's par for the course as they have neither morals nor ethical standards to begin with, at least I've yet to come across a politician with a conscience. Fortesque didn't introduce his bill into parliament out of an overwhelming fit of generosity, or because he thinks Mr Zheng is a good bloke. No, our Premier expects some remuneration for his troubles and Blakey's actions put such recompense on the backburner, at least until the bill has been passed. I have no doubt Fortesque would certainly have been a bit irate with Blakey, maybe enough to remove him from the land of the living.'

'Seems like the Bard was right when he said "there is nothing either good or bad, but thinking makes it so,"' Simon conceded, 'and having thought about it, it sure doesn't look good.'

Noel idly stirred his unsugared coffee. 'You know, this is all pretty heavy stuff,' he said. 'I thought we were investigating a simple murder, not an international conspiracy to commit whatever it is they might be planning to commit. And as Louisa said, there are any number of women all with a motive to commit murder, and all having the same intended victim.'

Simon nodded his agreement. 'Yep, and speaking of the dead, don't forget Robert Porter's murder is still unsolved, despite Rosetta's assertions, and he jilted more women than I've had Sunday lunches. And one of those jilted women was Monica Sainsbury-Ackerman, the wife of the Deputy Premier who probably got rid of her halfway up the bloody Amazon.'

'Aah, the undignified, morbid, grisly world of politics; wouldn't change it for quids,' Ron lamented. 'Anyway, boss, what's the next move?'

'City Council appears to be adopting a wait and see policy, at least as far as GPD's conceptual plans go. Graham's a little concerned that Gem might be providing council with an incentive to delay the GPD paperwork while pushing everything that needs pushing to facilitate Mr Zhang's whims. Although a visit to council might shed some light on the current situation, the murder of that bureaucrat Boswell at the Bondi Council offices, and the fact that all councils are full of would-be bureaucrats, I have no burning desire to visit City Council or any other council for that matter. However, I think it might be an idea to have a little heart to heart with Daniel Dawkins before we decide on further action.'

Chapter 19

The location for the meeting between the two detectives and
Daniel Dawkins was a decision made solely by Daniel. As his
nominated location happened to be the ocean promenade of
Manly beach, neither Simon nor Noel were willing to offer an
alternative, both more than happy to comply with Daniel's
venue ruling. It might have been a bit different had it been
pouring with rain, but it wasn't. The warm early morning sun
climbed lazily out of the blue horizon into a cloudless sky as
the gentle waves of the Pacific seemed in no particular hurry
to make it to the golden, sandy, beach. The only drawback, at
least to Noel's estimation, was that every half-naked nubile
body lazing on the beach enjoying the early morning
sunshine, or the skimpily clad fitness fanatics jogging along the
promenade, would have immediately identified the two men
attired in suit and tie for what they were; the police, and here
on business.

It was Noel who first sighted the lone gentleman staring
morosely out to sea while sitting on a bench under the Norfolk
Island pines. As the gentleman was in the agreed meeting
place, the assumption was made that here was Mr Daniel
Dawkins. However, the gentleman in question failed dismally

to fit either Noel's expectation of meeting the well-dressed businessman or the description provided by Ron Lange. Dressed in a garish Hawaiian floral shirt and a pair of shorts that must have been several sizes too large for the current wearer, the picture didn't quite meet that of the dapper and confident property developer, as painted by Ron.

'Daniel Dawkins?' Simon asked as he presumptuously sat in expectation of the affirmative response while noting a rather severe bruise on Daniel's leg.

'Yes, yes it is. Thanks for your time, Chief Inspector Webster,' Daniel replied as he remained seated to greet the two detectives. 'Mr Lange mentioned you and Sergeant Elliott might like to have a chat. In view of what has transpired lately, and as I am a little perturbed as to what I expect will happen in the future, I thought it time to lay my cards on the table and have a little chit-chat.'

'And just what seems to be the reason for your unease?' Simon enquired.

'Well, for starters there's the death of that politician bloke. While I had nothing to do with it, it just seems a little too close to home to pretend it didn't happen,' Daniel explained.

'Hey, hang about. Maybe you should start at the beginning,' Simon suggested. 'It seems his death might have resulted from the fact that he had upset a few people, including yourself.'

'Okay, but it's not a short story so you'll have to bear with me.'

'WELL, DO YOU BELIEVE HIM, BOSS?' Noel asked as he ceased typing up the notes from his notebook and, with an exaggerated theatrical movement of his right index finger, stabbed the "Save" key on his computer.

Simon, at the other end of the office, pursed his lips while he considered the blunt question. 'I think there are some things that have a ring of truth about them although I have yet to come across a squeaky-clean developer. I'll accept our Mr Dawkins has been in cahoots with Clyde Fortesque, and by association David Zheng, for the mutual benefit of all three, but whether that arrangement still holds good is debatable. According to Dawkins, Gem Development receive government contracts without having to tender which tends to confirm what Rosetta had to say. With grossly inflated cost to government, Gem, or Jezebel Dawkins, was able to provide substantial remuneration to those responsible for providing Gem with lucrative contracts in the first place, i.e. the Premier, or one of his minions.

'But before we go any further, we're investigating a murder, not the hankie-panky politicians and developers get up to. But don't get me wrong. I think their hanky-panky can pose a far more insidious, deliberately planned and long term illegal con on the tax payers than most murderers who, in most cases, act on a spur of the moment impulse.'

'Yes, I know,' Noel replied, 'but one thing leads to another and both Clyde Fortesque and Daniel Dawkins had motive for doing away with Morton Blakey. If Rosetta had any inkling of Morton's plan to cross the floor, one thinks she would have advised the Premier of his intention. Now, if Fortesque could see the ramification of his bill being defeated as a result of what Morton had in mind, he might have taken Morton out of play and delayed introduction of the bill until a compliant replacement had been found. To me it suggests Fortesque was completely unaware of Blakey's intention and was happy for the vote to be taken. Whether he was involved in Blakey's death out of sheer revenge is anybody's guess.'

'But what you're really saying is that Fortesque could have killed Blakey as he had the motive but didn't as there wasn't much point in doing so after the bill had been defeated,'

Simon said. 'Okay, seeing you seem to have all the bases covered, what of Dawkins and Zheng?'

Noel countenance took on one of earnestness; his boss wanted his opinion. 'No doubt both Fortesque and Dawkins are anticipating some financial remuneration from Zheng which won't happen until the foreign ownership problem has been cleared up. We know Zheng isn't averse to slipping the occasional financial incentive to those who are in a position and able to provide the required support. His problem at the moment is that he expects to see some positive results which have been stalled by Blakey's action. Despite the current hiccup, I think Clyde Fortesque has already received a retainer from Zheng and used it for a holiday with his secretary.'

Simon shrugged and gave a nod of agreement. 'But that means you believe Blakey's murder was predicated solely on the outcome of the Taipan Club debacle. I get the idea Graham Lee is the only person on the planet who didn't want to see Blakey dead as Blakey's action would turn out to be financially beneficial to Lee. At least he could then proceed with the GPD and the residential plan. But given all the political interference into Graham's simple redevelopment scheme, we may be overlooking a far more sinister motive for shoving a knife into Blakey's back. Dawkins certainly painted a pretty dismal picture of the personal relationships of the people implicated in the case, and they're not all politicians.'

'You mean the shenanigans he mentioned, including his own affair with Rosetta?' Noel queried.

'Okay, let's see. First off, you have Rosetta Blakey who knew Morton was screwing around with Jezebel, notwithstanding she and Daniel were at it as well. Irrespective of whatever Rosetta herself was up to, she wanted to be rid of the worm of a husband, as she put it, probably so she could concentrate on making Daniel husband number three. Considering she might have done away with her first husband, though I doubt it, we'll assume she has the propensity for permanently eradicating any source of irritation. Obviously, Morton couldn't have been so naïve not to know that he had become a pain in the neck to Rosetta, not that I think he really cared two hoots about Rosetta's feelings. Although Rosetta makes it sound like she was the one hard done by, I get the idea her affection for hubby, or lack thereof, was reciprocated. Morton's revelation that he didn't think she was worth two bob would have only exacerbated the mutual enmity between the two and would have done nothing to engender the possibility of any sort of reconciliation.

'Now, if we ignore any conspiracy or political implication that might exist between Daniel Dawkins and Clyde Fortesque, Daniel knew his wife was screwing around with a parliamentary backbencher named Morton Blakey who didn't know what side of the House he should be sitting. Meanwhile, it was while Jezebel was in the middle of this torrid affair that Blakey told her he would leave Rosetta and marry her. If she believed that it only confirms which of the seven dwarfs Jezebel is as he later unceremoniously dumped the poor misguided girl, probably after she got him elected to parliament. Depending on her emotional involvement with Blakey, the casting aside of his campaign manager might have pushed Jezebel a step too far. Whether that step would engender a hatred intense enough for her to stab him in the back then push him under a train can be answered only by one person, and that's Jezebel.

'Despite his claims of innocence, Jezebel's affair with Morton Blakey would have provided Daniel a motive for killing Blakey. By the same token, it probably provided him a good motive for killing Jezebel, but Jezebel's not dead, yet. To top all this off, Jezebel had reason for killing off both Daniel and Rosetta because of their little fling. Maybe Daniel's claim that Jezebel is in the process of poisoning him might be right.'

'Yeah, well when Sue and I were first married I thought she was trying to poison me as she wasn't the greatest cook on the planet although, I must admit, she has improved since then,' Noel confessed.

Noel's brief interruption to Simon's narrative failed to divert attention from the matter at hand with Simon totally preoccupied with the frailties of married life. 'Despite all the acrimony being thrown around, it does seem a bit hypocritical for Daniel to take umbrage at his wife's shenanigans while he seemed quite amenable for his wife to compensate Clyde Fortesque for contracts he didn't have to tender for. To me, that's taking the art of pimping to a new level.

'Of course, there's always David Zheng. Whatever his motive for wanting to build a six-star hotel might be, his plans have been thrown into disarray by Blakey's action. No doubt our Mr Zheng expected a smooth ride for the passing of a simple bill to allow overseas ownership of the property. When Blakey did what he did he certainly provided Mr Zheng a motive for getting himself permanently removed from the electoral role.'

Noel pushed his chair back from his desk, stretched his legs out in front of him and folded his arms. 'Okay, boss, so it boils down to the murder being either politically motivated based on pure greed, or murder inspired by the lustful pursuits of a few people driven by nothing more than their prodigious sexual appetite. That puts Clyde Fortesque, Daniel Dawkins and David Zheng in the first category with Rosetta Blakey, and both Jezebel and Daniel Dawkins in the second. I don't know what impression you had of Dawkins over at Manly, but to me he looked like death warmed up and about to kick the bucket. Whatever his lustful appetite or libido is at the moment, I doubt he would have the energy to do anything about it, poor sod.'

'Yes, he did look a bit seedy but maybe he always looks green around the gills,' Simon responded. 'And that bruise on his leg didn't look too healthy. But getting back to your list of suspects, you can include Zheng's travelling companion, John

Chang. Although I've never met the man, I have an idea he's one person I wouldn't like to meet in a dark alley. Which reminds me, anything back from overseas on Zheng?'

'Not as yet, and I'm not holding my breath.'

'I s'pose it's of little consequence as to who Mr Zheng is, or even what Mr Zheng is as the Premier seems to think the man's kosher,' Simon muttered dismissively.

'Yeah, well you'd think he was kosher too if he was paying you a bucket load of money for a bit of help to get what he wanted, and he wants the Taipan Club,' came Noel's snide response.

Simon's countenance took on a look of aggravated annoyance. 'See, we're doing it again,' he said as he rose from his chair, put his hands in his pockets and started to pace the floor. 'We know that developers, and the money men behind them, are constantly paying those in power for favourable decisions and those in power are more than willing to accept the financial benefits offered. Generally speaking, and I'll concede there must be the rare exception, with every development you see under construction you just accept the probability that someone is getting a kickback and that someone is more than likely to be a politician, from the lowly town councillor to state parliamentarian. But that's not our problem and although Blakey's murder might be linked to such immoral and unethical behaviour, it's our job to find the killer, not pass judgement on a bunch of unscrupulous developers or unconscionable politicians.'

Chapter 20

It wasn't often that Detective Superintendent Nigel Fisher had call to summon Detective Chief Inspector Simon Webster and his sidekick, Detective Sergeant Noel Elliott, to his office. Unbeknownst to Fisher, this seemingly innocuous act usually created a feeling of uncomfortableness and apprehension, an emotion shared by both detectives. Previous experience had shown that a summons to Fisher's office never seemed to fore-shadow anything in the way of good news and, invariably, was the harbinger of tidings both Simon and Noel could well do without.

Having dispensed with the somewhat cool preliminaries, the two detectives sat expectantly in front of Superintendent Fisher's ornate office desk. With Fisher firmly ensconced behind it and looking rather intimidating in the silver braided uniform, proceedings got underway. 'Well, gentlemen, I take it your investigation into the death of Morton Blakey hasn't produced any results, as yet?' he asked knowing full well the answer.

Simon shifted uncomfortably in his chair while Noel chose to adopt a far-away look of detached indifference in the hope Simon would respond to the simple enquiry. 'No, sir, that's not quite true,' Simon said with a shake of the head. 'We are pursuing two lines of inquiry with both providing motive. The nature of Blakey's murder seems to nullify the means and opportunity aspects of the case as everyone has access to a knife of some sort, and everyone has access to an electric train station. Even then, the opportunity aspect is very iffy as you would have to have a knowledge of Blakey's commuting routine. As everyone knew where he worked, the murderer could have just followed him to whatever railway station and done away with him when the opportunity presented itself.'

Superintendent Fisher rested an elbow on the chair's armrest as he held his chin, the other arm resting lackadaisically over the back of the seat. 'I take it one of these lines of investigation pertains to Graham Lee's Taipan Club?'

Simon nodded. 'Yes, sir. There's a Mr David Zheng, a Chinese entrepreneur, or at least we think he's an entrepreneur, who wants to knock down the club and build a you beaut hotel while Graham wants to build a residential complex. Naturally there's a political involvement and that's where Blakey came into the equation - and ended up getting himself killed.'

'Yes, yes, I know all about that and Blakey's decision to vote against some bill in the House,' Fisher growled as he adopted a more aggressive posture by folding his arms. 'And you, Sergeant Elliott, took to asking the police in Hong Kong for information on Mr Zheng and his buddy, John Chang?'

Detecting a note of censure, Noel could do nothing to hide his embarrassment as his face flushed a brighter shade of red. 'Sir, I'm unaware of any restrictive protocols in place to prevent the seeking of information from anywhere as long as the request is pertinent to an investigation. As there seems to be very little information available here on Mr Zheng, who has become quite pally with Premier Fortesque, or on Mr Chang, I asked Hong Kong.'

'And I take it you're still waiting for a response, keeping in mind you're not seeking information from the British now?' Fisher asked.

'Yes, sir.'

'Well, maybe this will satisfy you curiosity,' Fisher said as he withdrew a document from his "Pending" basket and offered it to Noel. 'I received that from a senior officer, a superintendent first class in Hong Kong. I would recommend you both inwardly digest the contents and consider the implications. And although it's not up to me to tell you how to suck eggs, I might suggest you exercise at least some semblance of prudence and caution in any investigation involving your Mr Zheng, or Mr Chang.'

Noel, having read the document, passed it to Simon who, after scrutinizing the contents and some serious deliberation, raised his questioning eyes to the Superintendent. 'And are there any restrictions on the dissemination of this information? Like, can we tell Graham Lee just who, or what, he's up against?'

Fisher folded his arms and sat back in his chair. 'There's nothing to suggest the contents are confidential so, as long as you apply the need to know principle, yeah, go ahead. You might also like to let the Premier know just who he's sipping green tea with.'

'Oh, I've no doubts the Premier knows exactly who, but not necessarily what he's sipping green tea with. And I don't think he has a clue as to the organisation behind this overseas cartel.' Simon muttered.

———

'LOOK, BOSS,' Noel protested, 'I must be one of the seven dwarfs, and no guessing for which one. I thought we were chasing up a murder case that now seems to be fading into insignificance just because of some skulduggery over a gambling casino, an illegal one at that. So, who cares if the

Premier is mixed up with Mr Zheng. We know the casino will be sold off to some overseas buyer, like every other property in the county with a "For Sale" sign attached to it. Now we're embroiled in a bit of alleged real estate hanky-panky, the murder of a prominent politician gets shoved onto the back-burner. Whether there is or isn't a shonky involving the Premier, our interest into the activities of Mr Zheng will cause the do-gooders out there to scream blue bloody murder, if, or when, they find out we're investigation the activities of someone from overseas. That's racial discrimination or xeno-phobia, no matter if the person of interest turns out to be Jack the bloody Ripper.'

Simon swivelled to and fro on his rickety chair. 'Oh, tetchy today, aren't we?' he responded. 'Just because the boss had a go at you doesn't mean you have to get stroppy with me. Whether you like it or not, everything is tied up with Blakey's murder and, to be honest, we haven't that many suspects to choose from.'

'Well, I reckon if Mr Zheng felt he had been metaphori-cally backstabbed by Blakey, he might have thought Blakey had given him enough motive to backstab him literally,' Noel, reposed on his chair, legs outstretched and hands in his pock-ets, countered.

'Granted,' Simon replied, 'but if that's the case, Zheng might hold Fortesque responsible. But I somehow get the feeling Zheng has an ulterior motive for wanting the Taipan Club, as we've already spoken about. The cost of the club would amount to a mere pittance and loose change for Zheng's backers. A six-star hotel would be peanuts in the greater scheme of things for those Hong Kong blokes. Now, if it came with a twenty seven hole golf course, an up-market boutique shopping centre and a gambling casino to go with it, it might be another matter as it would be a stand-alone finan-cial proposition. No, they probably want the place as a laun-dromat for their ill-gotten booty gained from scams perpetrated on poor unsuspecting plebs. I suppose that means I'm starting to come around to your way of thinking. Money from illegal operations, drugs, gambling, prostitution, et cetera, would have to be decontaminated through some apparent legal source and a hotel would fit the bill admirably.'

The ponderings over the inimitable Mr Zheng were bought to an abrupt halt as Simon, distracted from his train of thought, grudgingly responded to the ringing of his phone. With the meagre information gleaned from Simon's half of the conversation and the expression on his boss' face, Noel surmised something was amiss and that he would soon be apprised of some particularly unpleasant news.

On completion of the call, Simon pushed his chair back from the table and clasped his hands behind his head. 'Bugger,' he exclaimed in aggravation. 'That was Fisher, blast him. It seems we now have fewer contenders for Blakey's murder.'

'Hang on,' Noel interrupted, 'there's my phone,' he said as he picked up the receiver. Having been subjected to a bit of Noel's eavesdropping, it was now Simon's turn to eavesdrop on a one-sided conversation which, he gathered from the occasional word and Noel's demeanour, was causing Noel some considerable anxiety.

After a short exchange, Noel replaced the receiver, sat back on his chair and took a deep breath which he exhaled with a silent whistle. 'Well, I'll be…who would've thought,' he said in stunned astonishment. 'Okay, boss, looks like I have to agree with you on the number of contenders for the Blakey murder.'

Chapter 21

That the news of David Zheng's death was unforeseen and came as a bit of a surprise could be considered an understatement. However, news of the recovery of a body reported to be that of Rosetta Stone-Blakey from Sydney Harbour coupled with the reported death of Mr Zheng, both suspected of a possible involvement in the death of Morton Blakey, proved sufficiently coincidental to infuse a certain degree of consternation within both detectives. In fact, neither Simon nor Noel were overly impressed that the two victims had taken leave of planet Earth with many questions relating to the murder of Morton Blakey remaining unanswered. While Rosetta had seemingly co-operated when questioned, the opportunity to interrogate Mr Zheng had not presented itself and, in view of circumstances, was not likely to do so anytime within the foreseeable future.

'So, who told you about Zheng?' Noel asked.

'The Operations Room took a call last night advising of a blue between two men down in the Haymarket. When police arrived, they found a man slumped against the wall of a building with blood sprouting from a knife wound in his neck. Ambulance raced him off to hospital but he was dead on arrival. A crime scene squad led by Sergeant Canning from here went over to check out the location of the attack but there's nothing startling to reveal, not even CCTV coverage,' Simon replied. 'And how about your body?'

Noel gave a noncommittal shrug. 'An early morning fisherman over at Rushcutter Bay thought it was his lucky day until he landed his catch. He was all excited about his big fish until he saw what he had on the end of his line. Apparently when he recognised what it was, he threw up. Graham Gallymore attended following a request from Kings Cross Local Area Command. He made the connection with the Morton Blakey case as soon as a tentative ID of the body had been made. It was Gally on the phone just then. He'll get back to us with the when and the how once he's completed his poking around.'

Simon rested his elbow on the table, covered his eyes with his hand and slowly shook his head. 'Bloody hell, although there's no positive ID on either body, we'd better get something worked out what to tell Fisher. He'll go ballistic when he hears about this, if he hasn't done so already.'

Noel stood, planted his hands in his trouser pockets and scrutinised the white-board before he took up a red marking pen and put a neat single line through the names of Rosetta and Zheng. 'You know, boss, something is going horribly wrong here as we started off with only a few suspects and we have even fewer now. We're only left with Daniel and Jezebel Dawkins and Clyde Fortesque who I think we can discount.'

'Not necessarily so,' Simon returned. 'The only person we can eliminate as a murderer is Morton Blakey as he was the first to shuffle off this mortal coil. Rosetta or Zheng might have carried out a dastardly deed before they got themselves into a pickle. And don't forget, Graham Lee probably had a motive to kill off Zheng as he stood to lose a bucket of money if Zheng got his way. But we are being terribly presumptuous. We haven't a positive ID on either body and it won't be until we get Gally's reports as to whether they were the target of a homicide, committed suicide or were cases of accidental death. I take it Gally will take a look at the Haymarket body?'

'Yes,' Noel replied, 'he said he'd have a look at it once he's had a squiz at the harbour lady, although he did say a knife in the neck sounded an odd way to commit suicide and extraordinary bad luck for it to have been an accident.'

'What really peeves me,' Simon said, 'is we never did get to talk to Zheng. Here he was a suspect in the Blakey murder and an antagonistic twerp stuck in Graham Lee's craw, and we didn't even get to meet the bloke. And just where was John Chang while Zheng was getting knifed? You can bet your life Fisher's going to ask some awkward questions and I don't have any answers. Anyway, they say attack is the best defence, so let's get up there before he demands our presence.'

———

'WELL, ISN'T THIS JUST DANDY,' Superintendent Nigel Fisher, attired in mufti minus a jacket and still able to look the epitome of high fashion, crowed as the two detectives entered his office. 'I had the idea of inviting you up here to discuss certain events that I'm led to believe have come to pass within the last few hours. Fortunately, I curbed my enthusiasm and decided to see just how long it would take you two mental giants of the constabulary to recognise the gravity of the situation, if the certain events as reported prove to be factual. And by all means, please be seated.'

'I take it you are referring to the reports of a couple of bodies recovered from different parts of the city?' Simon asked tentatively in an effort to de-escalate the superintendent's "grave" situation.

A fleeting wry smile crossed Fisher's face. 'And these two bodies have nothing to do with the case currently under investigation?'

Simon's countenance took on one of unexpected surprise. 'Sir, the only investigation currently in progress is the murder of Morton Blakey. As the two overnight bodies are yet to be positively identified, it would be presumptuous to make any connection. I'll concede there is a possibility that the female body belongs to Rosetta Stone, or Rosetta Blakey, and there's the distinct possibility the body from down at the Haymarket belongs to David Zheng. Until there's positive ID, we're working on the belief the bodies may be connected, but not taking it as gospel.'

'Okay, let's assume, for argument sake, the bodies are those of whom we think they are,' Fisher conjectured. 'Although we have a where, and Doc Gallymore will tell us the how and when, we seem to be short of the whys. We can discount any involvement by Morton Blakey into the death of the victim currently thought to be Rosetta Blakey, which would have been a case of uxoricide if he had killed her, but seeing he was already dead I think we can discount his involvement. I don't know much about Morton and I know even less of Rosetta, apart from the fact that they were in a relationship akin to that you could expect from a mongoose and a cobra. Come to think of it, I know very little about this Mr Zheng either, apart from him being a member of some triad organisation and his attempt to buy into the city's commercial real estate market.'

Simon heaved a sigh in exasperation. 'Sir, as far as David Zheng goes, and not wishing to cast aspersions upon the dead, I believe he was a gangster of the worst type and we're probably better off without him. Although I never met the man, my opinion is based on the fact that he must have been a shrewd, shifty character. According to the Premier, Zheng was courteous in his dealings and, despite what I hear, acted in a completely gentlemanly manner. Obviously, he had ingratiated himself with our venal Premier in expectation of gaining his support, at a price, to secure Graham Lee's property.

'Although highly speculative, I have an idea our illustrious Premier used the proceeds of such ingratiation to whiz his secretary off to some remote island for a bit of hanky-panky. You can bet he saw the need to spend the cash before his wife got hold of it and news of the payment got out, which it probably will sometime in the future. After all, he's never going to admit to having received any inducement for the favourable treatment of some sneaky entrepreneur who just happened to be a member of some Chinese triad organisation.

'No, the only people I can think of who might have had reason to slit Zheng's throat would be Graham Lee or Henry Haines and I don't think either has the propensity to murder anyone despite both being financially disadvantaged by Zheng's efforts to take control of the Taipan Club.'

'Oh yeah. Well, although I'm not the one doing the investigation, how about that developer over at Bondi Junction, Henry Higgins?' Fisher growled. 'From where I sit, he stands to lose more than anyone else in this venture. He would have regarded Morton Blakey as an ally, while this Chinese bloke, the Premier and Gem Development, the enemy.'

Simon cast a searching glance to Noel who remained impassive to the Superintendent's not so illogical comments despite the use of Henry's inexact surname. After readjusting his uncomfortable seating position, Simon ventured forth. 'Yes sir, I've just mentioned Henry Haynes. I haven't spoken to Henry yet but from his previous involvement in cases we've investigated I'm of the opinion he's not involved in any homicidal activity, despite his cantankerous and belligerent attitude to life in general. Sure, he stands to lose a bundle and has already spent oodles in preparing the conceptual plans for every bureaucratic authority on the planet, but whether he's miffed enough to go on a killing rampage, I very much doubt. More interestingly, we have had a long discussion with Daniel Dawkins from Gem Development and have concluded that he is up to his neck in property development scams involving people within the political arena. Whether these scams have anything to do with the murder of three people is open to speculation and is subject to further investigation.'

'And what about the woman, Rosetta Blakey, who had herself kidnapped but wasn't? And I still haven't figured out why Morton didn't want us to investigate the incident as he was unaware it was a sham dreamt up by Rosetta,' Fisher continued.

'Maybe he thought any investigation into his private life might dredge up something he would prefer not to be dredged up, if you get my drift, sir,' Simon responded with a coy look.

'Meaning?'

'Just an unsubstantiated report that he and his campaign manager were an item at one time. As for Rosetta Blakey, and despite her death, she is still a person of interest in regards to the deaths of both of Morton and her previous husband, Alvin Stone. And this gets back to the question; is our plethora of recent dead bodies bound up with property development or are they affairs of the heart?'

Superintendent Nigel Fisher's demeanour was undergoing a metamorphosis which didn't bode well for the two detectives. 'Gentlemen, you are the investigators and it's your job to find the answers to your dim-witted questions; so, don't ask me. As it is, I have the distinct impression your investigation is coasting along without too much enthusiasm for getting positive results. Now, if you don't want to be pounding the midnight shift up at The Cross, or working as lollypop plods at the local kindergarten, you'll get out there and show a bit of interest. After all, we have three dead bodies, one of whom belongs to a politician, one the wife of the said dead politician and the third a respected businessman from the country that now owns half our own bloody country.'

Noel, aggrieved by Fisher's outburst yet maintaining some respect for rank, responded almost belligerently. 'Sir, while we would very much like to get on with it, you will appreciate the fact that current evidence suggests the possible involvement of politicians.'

'I don't give a brass razoo who you're dealing with, Sergeant Elliott,' Fisher brashly interrupted. 'If you have irrefutable evidence the man in the moon's taking kick-backs, go string him up. And that's an order.'

Chapter 22

'Well now, this is a fine kettle of fish you've got us into,' Simon scolded Noel with feigned indignation on return to their office. 'Like, just how do you get excited about venal politicians, unscrupulous developers and overseas gangsters loaded up with money trying to buy every bit of real estate they can get their hands on.'

'My sentiments exactly, but to be honest, boss, I'm beginning to wonder just who did what to whom, or is that to who?' Noel responded. 'Anyway, my interest has been piqued and I'd like to find out just what's happening, or has happened.'

Simon propelled his chair closer to his desk, took up a pen and opened his notebook. 'Okay, so let's crack on with it and comply with Fisher's directive, and to hell with the consequences. First up, get over to see Gally and find out where he's at with his post mortems. I don't care how preliminary the results are, but I want to know if Zheng and Rosetta met with foul play, although a knife in the neck suggests something is amiss. While you're doing that, call in at the station up at the Cross. Dave Harris is still up there so he should be able to give you a run-down on Rosetta's death. I expect his mob will have done a crime scene investigation on *Gemini* seeing it's moored at Rushcutter Bay, which is in Dave's bailiwick. In the meantime, I'm going over to see Henry Haynes and find out just what his involvement is, and has been, in the Taipan Club debacle. After all, Fisher is right when he says Haynes had motive to do away with Zheng although he probably had a better reason to do away with Daniel Dawkins, and he ain't dead, yet.'

'And what about Clyde Fortesque?' Noel asked.

'Meaning?'

'Well, if Clyde was taking kickbacks from Mr Zheng for government support in his bid for foreign ownership of a block of land in the middle of the city, and Mr Zheng manages to get himself terminated before anything is finalised, old Clyde Fortesque might be a bit miffed, to say the least. It would be interesting to find out just how Clyde is feeling at the moment.'

'Yeah, but don't forget, our Premier has just spent a bundle of money taking his secretary, whatsaname, on a junket to the South Pacific, maybe in the expectation there was more easy cash on the way. But let's not get ahead of ourselves so let's get the ball rolling,' Simon declared.

SIMON'S RECOLLECTION of Henry Haynes was that of a man with a chip on his shoulder and nothing less than an ill-tempered sod unable to display any vestige of civility. Mind you, the beating he took probably didn't do anything to moderate his disposition, and it didn't take Simon long to reinforce his previous perception of Henry's temperament. The Glover Property Development office, from which Henry worked, was located at Bondi Junction in the eastern suburbs of Sydney and was far from being the showcase shopfront for a successful property developer. But Henry couldn't care less. He was out to make money for both Ralph Glover and himself and therefore didn't need any of the aesthetic office trappings.

Simon sat back and made himself as comfortable as one could on a collapsible metal chair and, having decided there was no point in beating around the bush, launched into the object of the visit. 'Okay Henry, correct me if I'm wrong but with the untimely death of David Zheng I can't see any hurdles in the way of Graham Lee's residential project. The question I'm led to ask now is, did you have to eliminate the competition to get what you wanted?'

Henry Haynes did not move a muscle as he sat behind his paper strewn table with empty MacDonald's coffee mugs aplenty attesting to Henry's caffeine addiction. 'Bloody hell, and you call yourself a copper. If I was going to do away with anyone, it would have been that ratbag Dawkins. Sure, Zheng was the head honcho buying support for his project from wherever he could, and that included the Premier who's as crooked as a dog's hind leg and a nasty piece of work.'

'So, if you didn't kill Zheng, who did?'

'And how the bloody hell would I know, but when you find out let me know and I'll buy whoever it was a coffee,' Henry said in a rare display of benevolent generosity.

'Okay, let's start again. Who killed Morton Blakey?'

'And again I say, you're the copper. You tell me. If you think I had anything to do with that, you're nuts. Mr Blakey was on my side, or Mr Lee's side. He was dead set against Zheng's foreign ownership application and was vehemently opposed to the selling off of any of the country's asset to overseas buyers. Mind you, Blakey was a voice in the wilderness. Although he crossed the floor to vote with the opposition to defeat the Foreign Ownership Bill, the opposition voted against it for no other reason than the bill was government sponsored, certainly not for any altruistic motive. In reality, no-one gives a damn who owns what, at least the politicians don't. As long as they're suitably remunerated, they couldn't give a stuff who supplies the kickback, and it's generally the members within government who get the big bikkies as they're in a position to make the decisions.'

'Well, don't look now, but you're a developer. Don't tell me you don't pay the odd politician or local government functionary some compensation for favourable consideration?' Simon argued.

Henry pressed his lips together and slowly shook his head before responding. 'DCI Webster, it's actions you probably consider immoral, illegal, unprincipled or unethical that makes the world go round, a fact that is certainly not lost on politicians. I would venture to say there's not a politician alive, anywhere, who's in the game to render his constituents a magnanimous and public-spirited service. While they try to appear to us peasants as being selfless, charitable and kind-hearted pillars of society, in reality all they have to do is sit on their bums and wait for the myriad of unethical financial opportunities to come along for nothing more than a nod of the head. And as you're probably unaware of just what is going on, why do you think the price of real estate is higher than a public servant's ego?'

Simon pursed his lips as he considered the question no-one had been able to provide a credible answer to. 'Okay, Henry, you're the developer; you tell me.'

'Simple,' replied Henry. 'It all comes down to the mighty dollar and the principle of supply and demand. The big developers make sure that the demand always outstrips supply by withholding projects until they know the demand for residential sites has far outstripped the supply available. The consequence of this little farce is to force up the price of what's already available. That's when the developers will complete a project and release more residential sites onto an already highly inflated market; hence more profit to the developer. And local councils are only too pleased to see grotesque high-rise development squeezed into every available block of land.

Whereas a block of land might provide council with half a dozen rate payers, a high-rise development on the same block of land could mean hundreds of rate payers. And what comes onto the market is usually bought up by cashed-up overseas buyers who give the Aussie battler no chance at owning his own home. Naturally, there's always the initial under the table transactions to establish the groundwork for further negotiations between politicians and developers, to their mutual financial advantage, of course. And don't get me wrong. This practice extends from state to local government politicians and bureaucrats all reaping the rewards, which stinks. Every time I see a crane on the skyline, I wonder which politician has his nose in the trough.'

Simon, acknowledging the rather comprehensive insight of Henry's perception of reality, pursed his lips and gave a gentle nod of the head. 'Well, now you've cleared that up, I think you've failed to answer the question; are you in the habit of remunerating bureaucrats for favourable treatment?'

A surprised look came over Henry's face. 'Humble apologies, DCI Webster, but I thought you were making a statement, not posing a question. However, I will concede the answer is a "sometimes", depending on the situation, not that I think GPD could be construed as a large developer. Sure, Gem Development may fall into that category as they certainly try to manipulate the number of projects going on around the place. And David Lee's idea of a residential complex in the heart of the city would be totally contrary to the best interests of the big developers. And no, I didn't compensate Morton Blakey for his petulance in crossing the floor, for which I'm grateful. He was one of the few good guys and I'm sorry to see him dead.'

'Okay, but what's your attitude towards Dawkins, considering the current circumstances, and with Dawkins applying for an injunction to prevent sale of the Lee's property?' Simon asked.

Henry screwed up the waste paper from a Big Mac and squeezed it into an empty coffee mug. 'And that's the sixty four thousand dollar question. Zheng was working for a conglomerate and had already paid out quite a substantial amount of money for support, including a nice little retainer to Mr Dawkins. Dawkins had no reason to kill Zheng as Zheng was the goose that laid the golden egg, for Dawkins anyway. I have no idea just where the ball will fall now as I'm sure the Premier still sees the hotel development a means to riches with kickbacks, probably from Zheng's mob, and from Gem; Zheng's mob because they want the place for a hotel and Gem because Dawkins wants the Premier's political support to have Lee's residential proposal trashed so he can get on with Zheng's hotel.

'Dawkins probably thinks there's quite enough developers whacking up apartment blocks in the city already without Mr Lee adding to the supply side of the equation. He can't do anything about the demand side of things, which will continue to grow, so he'll continue to manipulate the supply side, in collusion with other developers. Obviously, the aim of this little exercise is to drive residential prices further into the realm of fantasy for the majority while catering for the bucket loads of money foreign investors are more than happy to part with.

'Dawkins' injunction application is still before the court and I have no doubt the Premier will try to influence whichever court has to decide on that issue. It's my guess the presiding judge will order a stay of proceedings until the overseas investment issue is decided. The uncertainty at the moment is whether someone takes over from Zheng to pursue the hotel scheme, or the Foreign Ownership Bill gets scrapped all together. So really, DCI Webster, there's stuff all Graham Lee or I can do until the dust has settled.' And with that, Henry relegated the McDonalds coffee mug to the waste bin.

WHILE IT HAD BEEN some time since Detective Sergeant Noel Elliott had met with Chief Inspector Dave Harris of the Kings Cross Local Area Command, his recollection of the ageing crime fighter had not been altered by the passage of time. Dave Harris, his white hair maybe a little thinner, still maintained a friendly face while his soft blue eyes belied the true nature of the experience toughened police inspector.

'Well, if it ain't DS Elliott, and without his boss, even,' Inspector Harris declared as he stood to greet his colleague while indicating to the vacant chair in front of his desk. 'Doc Gallymore said I could expect a visit from somebody from Day Street. Seems the lady fished out of the harbour was the wife of the recently eliminated politician, or should I say the recently obliterated politician.'

'Yes, a rampant train can do that to you, if you're not careful,' Noel said in agreement, 'and yes, seeing his wife was fished out of the pond in your bailiwick, and as you're doing the investigation, we'd like any info that may help to find the culprit responsible for both is and her death.'

'Fair enough, but maybe we should pool our resources to find out who did Mrs Blakey in,' Harris suggested as he reached for a buff coloured file from his "In" tray.

'Sounds good to me,' returned Noel. 'There's enough motive for killing Morton Blakey to sink a battleship, but Rosetta is a different kettle of fish.'

Inspector Harris handed Noel the file and sat back as Noel scanned the few pages already collated into the death of Rosetta Blakey. 'I don't know if Doc Gallymore has been in touch with you yet, but you'll find his preliminary report in there somewhere. Seems Rosetta drowned, which is a bit unusual as most people can swim enough to save themselves. Maybe she was one of the ones who couldn't. But there again, there were some minor injuries to her head and upper body together with the presence of a boathook with traces of her hair attached. This suggests she was thrown overboard and kept there by being prodded with the boathook by person, or persons unknown until she couldn't continue to struggle any longer.'

'I'm off to see Gally after I leave here so I guess I'll get all the gruesome details then. Is there any evidence of just who might have been aboard *Gemini* on the evening in question?' Noel asked.

Harris paused, sucked in his lips and gazed momentarily at the ceiling. 'We know Charlie Chambers, the deck hand, wasn't aboard that night, more's the pity. He went to see Souths get flogged by Manly at Redfern Oval and ended up staying the night at his mate's place following a bit of a knees up. During a search of *Gemini*, we located three wine glasses in various stages of emptiness in the saloon. As one had lipstick on it, we're of the opinion that that particular glass was being used by a visitor, probably a female visitor, although you never know these days. Forensics did a check of fingerprint records and there was no match which only means whoever was there hasn't come to police notice.'

'And did Rosetta have any traces of lipstick on her when they pulled her out of the harbour?' Noel asked.

'No, which suggests she might not have been expecting the visitors and hadn't gone to the trouble of donning a bit of makeup.'

'Sounds reasonable,' Noel conceded. 'And you think these two visitors, probably a male and a female, invited Rosetta up on deck, pushed her over the side and, with the use of a boathook, kept her there until she didn't come up. If that is how it was, I'd say the visitors knew Rosetta couldn't swim as it would have been easy enough to just paddle away if she could. One question I should have asked before we started; has Graham Lee been advised that his guest has done a bunk?'

'Sure has, but that's being a bit harsh. I'm sure Rosetta didn't have any say in the matter and would still be aboard *Gemini* if she was still alive and kicking,' replied Harris. 'Once we made the connection between the victim and *Gemini* we got in touch with Lee. He's very supportive and will give us any assistance we require. Unfortunately, the poor bloke feels that it doesn't do the reputation of his boat any favours now a murder has been committed onboard. I feel a bit sorry for Mr Lee as I genuinely believe he hasn't a clue what's going on.'

Noel nodded in agreement. 'Well, he ain't on his Pat Malone there. And that Chinese entrepreneur bloke, trying to undermine Lee's plans for his residential complex, ends up extremely dead with his throat cut. But don't get me wrong, although that may appear to have provided Graham with a pretty good motive to do away with Zheng, I don't believe Graham is the murdering type. However, we reckon this sudden spate of murders are all connected. We just have to find out the whys and the wherefores and marry each victim up with their respective killer. The hows are the easy bit.'

Chapter 23

The atmosphere in Simon's office was not one of over exuberant enthusiasm. In fact, the three occupants of the office nurtured a fervent desire that the matter at hand would simply fade away into Einstein's ether. However, being realistic, Simon was well aware that his boss, Superintendent Nigel Fisher, probably harboured the view that the arrest and conviction of the perpetrator responsible for the dastardly murder of a prominent politician would be a career enhancing opportunity. And it was for sure that now the opportunity had presented itself, Superintendent Fisher would milk every bit of career mileage to be had out of the investigation, hence his not so subtle and emphatic "get on with the job" directive.

Simon had cynically thought it somewhat ironical how the repute and stature of a lowly backbencher should suddenly rocket up the credibility ladder following the sudden intervention of the grim reaper, irrespective of the fact his colleagues openly detested the man and his vacillating whims. Nonetheless, as Morton Blakey had been done in by person or persons unknown, along with the death of his wife, Rosetta, in a totally separate incident, an unusual amount of public interest had been generated by the press in their inimitable way of never letting the facts stand in the way of a good story. While there was much speculation being bandied about as to the identity of the guilty party, or parties, it was doubtful anyone really cared who the political assassin might be, and it would only be a matter of days before both public and press interest would be as dead as the victims themselves.

'Okay Noel, and just what information have you extracted from Dave Harris?'

'Not much,' Noel replied after he stretched his legs out in front of himself, lounged back and folded his arms. 'Dave gave us a copy of the file and suggested we take over the investigation in view of Rosetta's connection with Morton.'

'Yeah, I s'pose there is a connection there somewhere, seeing they were married,' Simon replied cynically. 'And what little snippets of gossip was Gally able to provide?'

'Well, Rosetta's death is certainly a case of murder. He seems to think that however she got herself into the harbour, someone wanted to make sure she wasn't going to get out. She had some minor injuries to her head, not enough to do any damage but enough to keep her in the water. Seems the poor girl couldn't swim and no-one was overly anxious to pull her out. In fact, evidence suggests someone used a boathook to make sure she wasn't going to remain on the surface for too long. The big question is motive. There's nothing that comes to mind, at least not with hubby already dead.'

Having sat listening to the two detectives and totally engrossed in their trivial revelations that, according to his assessment, amounted to very little, Ron felt that somewhere there had to be a scrap of information of value to the investigation. 'Okay, Simon, and what momentous news from the cantankerous developer over at Bondi Junction?' Ron asked in expectation of something a little more substantial than trivial.

Simon pressed his lips together, raised his eyebrows and gave a non-committal shrug. 'All terribly enlightening stuff really, although nothing to write home about. Henry seems to think it's a case of developers manipulating the market to gain the biggest profits which is par for the course for any business, irrespective of the business being conducted. Obviously, the principle these days is to screw the plebs for every penny and not let ethics stand in the way of a bigger profit margin.'

'My, my, and what side of the bed did we get out of this morning, or did Georgie overwind your clock?' Ron asked in a rather condescending manner.

'Look, I'm getting a little cheesed off with the whole thing,' Simon said testily as he vented his frustration. 'So, we find the murderers of Morton Blakey, Rosetta Blakey and David Zheng. So what? Some judge would probably give the guilty whoevers two years jail and then suspend the sentence upon the whoevers entering into a two-year good behaviour bond.'

Somewhat taken aback by his boss's little outburst, Noel dared to voice his tuppence worth. 'I'm not saying I disagree with you, boss, but I find there is some satisfaction in working out who the criminals are. To try and rid the streets of villain, gangsters and thugs for altruistic motives is a waste of time as we can't even rid the streets of puppy poo, thanks to a judiciary hell bent on supporting those poor unfortunates who have, by their own choice, turned to a life of crime. We have to get our satisfaction from nothing more than bringing the baddies to justice. Whatever happens after that is beyond our control. Anyway, I'm for investigating the three murders, if for nothing more than to satisfy my own curiosity.'

'Well said,' applauded Ron, 'so let's get cracking and do a little investigating, and with some enthusiasm.'

'Okay, Ron, seeing you're all bright eyed, bushy tailed and enthusiastic to get this investigation revved up, what do you have in mind?' Simon asked as he lounged back on his very unstable office chair. Ron Lange, settled on the new but most uncomfortable office racing chair, a little surprised by Simon's simple question.

Ron cast a suppliant glance to Noel who was relaxing, sitting back with his feet resting on the desk with hands clasped together on his lap. Unfortunately, Noel's response to Ron's subtle plea for assistance in answering Simon's simple question amounted to nothing more than a shrug and a "damned if I know" look etched across his face. In an effort to regain some credibility, Ron bounced out of his chair and started pacing the floor, hands clasped behind his back in a posture oozing assertive authority and self-assurance, albeit a charade to hide the fact he didn't have a clue as to where he should start his little bit of investigating.

'Well, it appears to me that much of what we have covered so far has related to the murders of Morton Blakey and his wife, Rosetta. If you have nothing specific for me to follow up, Simon, I would suggest I chase up the murder of David Zheng and see just where his mate, John Chang, fits in. We seem to have taken a lot of interest in Zheng but nothing on Chang,' Ron expounded, quite pleases that he could come up with such an enlightened course of investigation on the spur of the moment.

'No, we haven't, that's true. Okay Ron, that sounds like a good idea,' Simon replied. 'Whoever John Chang is, he's travelling on a Chinese passport and is using an anglicised name. No doubt he has a drawer full of passports all in different names, but maybe I'm being a tad cynical. We know he relocated from Beijing to Hong Kong and he's a member of a triad thing. With the exit of the British from Hong Kong, and a strict Chinese government influence imposed, maybe the crime gangs are looking for greener pastures and, heaven knows, Australia has green pastures.'

Chapter 24

It had been some time since so many guests had been assembled on the back lawn of the bungalow at 24 West Bank Lane, Collaroy, located on Sydney's northern beaches. But as an accepted truism, circumstances generally tend to influence subsequent proceedings. It therefore followed that Simon was quite anxious to determine just what circumstances had already evolved and what might be realistically anticipated in the future so that suitable subsequent proceedings might be pursued should, or when, unforeseen events crop up. To put it in a nutshell, neither Simon nor Noel had much of an idea as to who was responsible for the three murders recently perpetrated. In view of Superintendent Fisher's directive to "get on with it", a spark of inspired police investigative work was urgently needed to provide some credible grounds for the reinstatement of lost confidence, or one Superintendent Nigel Fisher might very well have grounds for being a tad narky with his two detectives.

'Okay, people,' Simon said as he addressed the group, 'you may or may not have any idea as to what the object of this little exercise is. Firstly, most of you know each other, our two exceptions might be Alf and Benny who were probably responsible for starting off this little fiasco. Doubtless you are all aware of the demise of Morton Blakey and his ever-loving wife, Rosetta, along with the tragic death under suspicious circumstances of Mr David Zheng, a representative of an offshore consortium wishing to purchase property currently occupied as the Taipan Club. In view of our success, or lack thereof, I have invited you here for a brainstorming session as such sessions in the past have resulted in some notable, if not novel, success. So, let's kick off with the first death, that of Morton Blakey.'

'Well, as far as I'm concerned,' Alf said with conviction, 'Rosetta knocked him off. When she found out she wasn't worth a hundred bucks in ransom, she decided a divorce might only amass half the Blakey assets; far better to do away with the cretin and take all the assets.'

Simon nodded. 'Yes, we've considered that angle, but could she have stuck him in the back with a knife and then shove him out in front of a train? I'm pretty sure if she was involved in his murder, she would have to have had an accomplice. The only people we can think of who might fill that dubious position would be Daniel Dawkins, who has admitted to an affair with Rosetta, and David Zheng who really had an axe to grind with Mr Blakey. According to my time-line Zheng was alive and kicking when Morton was dispatched.'

'And oh, what a tangled web we weave', Judy drawled, a look of total disinterest etched across her freckly face. 'It sounds to me like everyone had a motive for doing away with someone or other. Jezebel had motive for doing away with both of the Blakeys and her own hubby, Daniel. Daniel had motive for doing away with Morton, and I couldn't care less who else he might have had motive to murder; so yes thanks, Ron, I will have another Chardonnay.'

'My, my, a bit tetchy today,' Ron responded as he obediently refilled Judy's glass.

Simon rested is chin in the palm of his hand and slowly shook his head. 'No, unfortunately I think I share Judy's sentiments, Ron. There seems to be no-one involved in this case who hasn't got themselves murdered already, or isn't about to be. I suppose there are a few candidates for the mortician still remaining and they would have to include Jezebel, Daniel, Premier Fortesque and, of course, there's you David. I'm inclined to think that somewhere within that list of names is our murderer, or at least one of them, so if we sit back the whole thing will sort itself out.'

'Gee, thanks,' Graham interjected. 'All I wanted to do was get rid of the Taipan Club and have Henry Haynes build an apartment block. I thought the whole idea all very reasonable, bearing in mind the economic plight of first-home home-buyers at the moment. And now you see me as a target for obliteration at the hands of some perverted murderer.'

'Hang about, Simon, when you say the thing will sort itself out, are you suggesting there are more murders to be had?' Louisa asked, somewhat perturbed of her husband's possible vulnerability of becoming another victim.

Simon shrugged before leaning forward to scoop a handful of peanuts from the small table arranged with assorted nibblies. 'While it's hard to establish a common motive for the demise of our trio, we may have to accept that there was more than one person involved and that these people, whoever they may be, had different motives for doing away with their respective victim.'

'Like, the Premier had a good enough reason for shoving Morton in front of a train because he wouldn't toe the party line?' Georgie, not too sure if the Premier of the state would be implicated in such a gruesome murder, queried.

'And that's the point Simon is making,' Noel said. 'While the Premier might have had motive for Morton's death, it seems unlikely he had anything to do with Rosetta's or Zheng's. Unfortunately, the operative words are "might have" as it's possible there was only one murderer with a motive, still unbeknownst to us, for doing away with the threesome.'

Ron, having just extricated the can of beer he was seeking from the bottom of the esky, turned to Noel with an enquiring look. 'It seems to me the name of David Zheng is conspicuous with its absence. Given the information received back from Hong Kong and the fact that Zheng was a member of one of the triad organisations, albeit fairly low on the ladder, I would think his demise shouldn't come as any great surprise as I suspect the life expectancy of a gangster to be a bit iffy.'

'So, what info did you come up with on Zheng's travelling companion, John Chang?' Simon asked.

'Not much,' Ron replied. 'I had a chat to a few contacts down in China Town's Dixon Street but no-one seems to know anything about Mr Chang. Everyone I spoke to was aware of Zheng and the fact he'd been murdered, but Mr Chang is an enigma. Hong Kong did confirm he is a triad member but keeps such a low profile nobody seems to know what he's about, except he'd been accompanying Zheng everywhere Zheng went. There are a number of rumours as to who, or what Chang might have been, from bodyguard to Man Friday or nothing more than Zheng's bag carrier. Irrespective of what Chang is, it's apparent a lot of people believe both Zheng and Chang are, or were, kosher, and that includes the Premier. I suspect old Fortesque would have been reluctant to admit to his dealings with them if he had any idea they were members of some triad clan.'

After a meaningful "harrumph", Simon cast Ron a sceptical glance. 'Holy hell, Ron, I thought you had come to accept the true character of the politician. There are many politicians on this earth who regard themselves as statesmen and take great effort to expound their virtues of being squeaky clean and the most honourable, ethical and trustworthy people on the planet. In fact, they go out of their way to promote this belief. If the truth be known, the time has long passed since a politician could legitimately lay claim to being a statesman endowed with such noble qualities. As masters of spin you should never accept what they say at face value as we have been subjected to so many blatant lies you never know who or what to believe.'

'Gee, sorry I mentioned the Premier,' Ron returned, 'but he's the only one we have, and you have to trust someone.'

'Yeah well, you trust our illustrious Premier and I'll trust Jack the Ripper, and seeing he's dead I'd still vote for him and not the bunch of idiots we have running the place at the moment,' Simon said. The thing that disturbed Ron, to some degree, was the fact that he was fully aware of Simon's vitriolic resentment of politicians was firmly entrenched in his mind. Yep, no love lost there, Ron thought.

Turning to Graham Lee, Simon asked the question many people sitting around the table of nibblies were anxious to be asked. 'Anyway, Graham, what's the current situation with the Taipan Club?'

Before replying, Graham, in a dismal display of vulgar affluence, gulped the remains of his Bin 707 Cab Sav. 'That, my good friend, is a question I would love to know the answer to. As far as I know, the injunction taken out by Gem is still valid as it made no reference to Zheng. It therefore looks like the Premier and the bloke from Gem, aah, Daniel Dawkins, will continue on their merry way, despite the demise of Zheng. I have heard Zheng's replacement is either already in country, or is on his way.'

Georgie looked at Simon with a look containing a mixture of forlorn hope and pleading. 'Come on, Simon, you have every right to question the Premier about Zheng's murder as he was in cahoots with Zheng himself. I'm sure you could bend the questioning around to ask about the Taipan Club just to see what the Premier's attitude towards the future of the club is. And this bloke, John Chang. He's keeping a low profile which suggest to me he's up to no good, if he hasn't been already. Being so conspicuous with his absence, he's the first person I would want to speak to as I bet he's involved in the acquisition of the Taipan Club.'

Chapter 25

'Excuse me, ma'am, but I'd like to see the Premier,' Simon said as he displayed his warrant card to the well-dressed lady behind the information counter of the State Office Block.

The well-dressed lady turned, surprising Simon with the transformation from the look of an ostentatious bohemian tart who usually occupied the counter, to a lady displaying considerable high fashion dress sense, and exuding an aura of charm and sophistication. So, little old Jackie certainly gives credence to the adage clothes maketh the man, or in this case the woman, Simon thought, quite taken aback with Jackie's new image.

'Well, Detective Chief Inspector Webster, I haven't seen you for a while so everything must be hunky-dory,' Jackie responded as she closed the visitors' register and pushed it to one side. 'By the same token, I suppose there are a few people I haven't seen around here lately.'

'Anyone in particular?' Simon asked, now a bit confused as to Jackie's transformation from the girl with the look and dress sense of someone you wouldn't want to take home to meet mum. In addition, his curiosity had been piqued by Jackie's simple statement relating to the absence of people she had obviously expected to see on a more frequent basis.

'Can't say I've seen much of that Chinese business man, Mr Zheng, although his shadow, you know, the bloke who was always with Mr Zheng, has called in on the Premier a couple of times. It seems he's calling instead of Mr Zheng, not that I'm privy to anything that goes on in the boss's office,' Jackie said as she settled herself on a high stool and crossed her legs at the ankles. 'Oh yes. There's another person who sometimes calls in with the Chinese gentleman.'

'Oh, that's interesting. And do tell. You know the name of this "other person"?'

After reaching for the visitor's register and flipping to the last few pages, Jackie drew her finger down the list of names before recognising the required entry. 'Aah yes. A Mr Daniel Dawkins of Gem Property Development.'

'My, my,' Simon responded, 'now, who would ever have believed that? And you have no idea as to the nature of the visit?'

'Only that I think it had something to do with whatever it was Mr Zheng was seeing the Premier about.'

'Hmmm, you're probably right. And for your own information, don't expect to see Mr Zheng in the foreseeable future.'

'Oh, and why is that, Chief Inspector Webster? Has Mr Zheng gone back to China or something?' Jackie asked as she closed the register.

'Yes, to the "or something", at least. Mr Zheng is now in the big fortune cookie jar in the sky, probably reading up on his future prospects, which don't appear too crash hot at the moment.'

'You mean...' Jackie asked with genuine consternation.

'Yep, knifed in the neck. Made it to hospital but never looked like recovering, which he didn't,' Simon explained. 'Anyway, before I see the boss, what's with the change?'

Simon asked, his gaze sufficient to convey his precise question.

Jackie sighed and clasped her hands together on the counter. 'I think I might have told you on an earlier occasion that I was going to write a book about this place and all the shenanigans that go on. Unfortunately, that idea has gone down the gurgler as I can't stand the place any longer. I'm not bucking for a merit award or anything like that, but I would like a decent reference to take with me. Somehow I don't think my previous presentation would have landed me a suitable reference for a job in a knock-shop up at The Cross.'

'And what's the straw that broke the camel's back?' Simon asked, intrigued now he had found someone else to share his pet aversion; politicians.

'Apart from the political correctness garbage that goes on, nothing in particular,' Jackie said matter-of-factly, 'just an accumulation of stuff, and if I wasn't the lady I am now, I would have said the accumulation of a load of crap. I can accept the obnoxious treatment dished out by the public who have this weird idea that just because I work here I must be a politician and therefore a font of knowledge. The politicians and bureaucrats who run the place, together with their egos, regard me somewhat differently. They see me as being intel-lectually bankrupt, mentally deficient, which I'm not, and treat me with nothing but patronising contempt. While they have this strange belief that they have risen to the realms of the aristocracy and qualified to sit in the House of Lords, every man and his dog knows that they do absolutely nothing for their own constituents. They would rather spend their time in exploiting the opportunities and privileges available to parliamentarians while making bucket loads of dubious money before they get voted out of office.'

'Gee, Jackie, sorry I asked, but I know where you're coming from. Look, I'd better get on and see the boss. You'll let him know I'm on my way?'

'HOLY MOLY, this is getting a bit out of hand. For your information, DCI Webster, I am the Premier of the state and am a very busy man. I've far better things to do than sit around and chew the fat with you.'

Unperturbed by the Premier's obvious antipathy towards his persistent visitations, Simon decided to dispense with the niceties of social etiquette and adopted a far more politically incorrect approach. After all, if the Premier chose not to regard the murder of one of his backbenchers as a serious matter that warranted a thorough police investigation, that was not Simon's fault.

'Mr Premier, in previous discussions relating to the murder of Morton Blakey, you have provided the name of David Zheng who, through your own admission, instigated your Foreign Ownership Bill into parliament.'

Simon's statement, being one of fact and made without any rhetorical pretence, did elicit a reaction from the Premier who shuffled uncomfortably in his chair before adopting a defensive posture, arms folded and a deep frown furrowed across his face. 'Yes, but I hear Mr Zheng has suffered an unfortunate accident which rules him out of taking any further participation in the Taipan Club takeover.'

Simon harrumphed and scratched the back of his head. 'Yes, one could say a fatal knife attack to the neck might have the tendency to curb anyone's inclination for further participation in anything. And as the press has kept the details of Mr Zheng's unfortunate demise to a minimum, may I ask how you became aware of his sudden departure?'

'Of course. His colleague, John Chang, visited my office and told me the news. It seems he'll be taking over the negotiations for the property.'

'So, Mr Zheng's untimely passing in no way impedes the objective of the little exercise?'

'Hell, no. I've gone to a lot of trouble already to assist this overseas concern with the purchase of a chunk of real estate,' the Premier declared emphatically.

'Yes, but we all know you're being well paid for your troubles.'

The Premier raised his eyebrows and gave a slight nod of the head. 'That, DCI Webster, is a slanderous accusation and if made outside this office, I would sue you.'

'Ahh yes, but it's not a slanderous accusation, if true. I take it Mr Chang is aware of the payment made to you by Mr Zheng?'

'Any payment that might, or might not have been made, has been made solely to reimburse me for expenses I have incurred. Mr Zheng was anxious to secure my support and I believed his plans for an up-market hotel would be of great benefit to both Mr Zheng's consortium and to the state; a win win situation. Needless to say, Mr Chang is fully aware of such payment, if the payment was ever made in the first place.'

Simon felt quite smug; he had the Premier on the run and giving answers only an experienced politician could dream up. 'Substantial amount?'

'What? Oh, you mean the amount of money paid, or not paid by Mr Zheng. Yes, quite substantial and more to come once the bill has been passed. However, having said that, DCI Webster, I reject the insinuation that I have received a gratuitous payment from anyone. In addition, I refuse to confirm or deny at this point of time if further payments will be made following the passing of the bill.'

Sitting back in the lounge chair in front of the Premier's grotesquely big office table, Simon, his elbows on the armrests, gently tapped his arched fingers together. 'Okay, forgetting the money side for the moment, the crux of the matter, Mr Premier, relate to the deaths of Morton Blakey, his wife Rosetta and David Zheng which are all connected and centred around the Taipan Club debacle. As you have a vested interest in proceedings, and are also linked to the victims, you have become what we refer to as "a person of interest".'

'Oh no, no, no. You're not pinning that wrap on me. As I've said, there's been nothing illegal with my dealing with the overseas concern. I admit I may have received compensation for out of pocket expenses but there's nothing illegal about that. Okay, so there are those people out in the community who may regard such financial arrangements unethical. Well, that may be the case, but I am a politician and I do have a long-standing tradition of unethical behaviour to uphold. On top of that, as Premier of the state, I can't afford the luxury of being involved in a multi-homicide investigation as it wouldn't bode well for my re-election chances. So, DCI Webster, now you know the whole story, I suggest you get on with your investigation into the unsolved murders while I get on with my job. In fact, I'm already late for a meeting with an overseas mining consortium who want an open cut coal mine in the Hunter Valley.'

Chapter 26

'Well, it's not often you favour us with your presence, Gally; must be something important,' Simon said as the doctor of forensic pathology placed his briefcase on a filing cabinet and glanced around the office. To be sure, it had been some time since Graham Gallymore had occasion to take the trip over to Day Street; after all, he was a very busy man and, for some unaccountable reason, getting busier with a seemingly endless supply of cadavers requiring his expert attention.

Gally sighed and gave a shrug. 'Look, you two policing prodigies, I'd be able to make the occasional social call if it wasn't for the amount of work I have piled up. What is it, three in the last few days, and all of 'em a bit sus to say the least.'

Noel gave a smile as he gently rocked back and forth on his chair. 'Yeah, but you've got the easy job of the how and when. We have to determine the why and find the guilty parasite of whom there seem to be ever-increasing numbers. So, Gally, what earth-shattering tidings do you have that's going to knock our socks off?'

Doctor Gallymore turned to his briefcase from which he extracted three large envelopes and handed them to Simon.

'They're the final reports of the three recent victims you've sent me.'

'Let's skip the technicalities and get to the nitty-gritty,' Simon said as he consigned the unopened envelopes to his "In" basket. 'Morton shoved in front of a train with a knife in his back, his wife fished out of the harbor deader than a temperance wine-tasting party and Zhengie with his throat looking decidedly the worse for wear.'

'And I get a decent pay packet for poking around and putting bodies back together to see what terminated them. Hell, what a waste of time and money as you blokes have all the answers,' Gallymore said as he seated himself on the seldom used new office chair.

Simon slowly shook his head. 'Sorry, Gally, but basically we haven't a clue as to what's going on. So far, our investigations have had as much success as a chihuahua would have in that Alaskan doggy race, not that I can recall a chihuahua having ever been entered.'

Gally chuckled to himself and, with a nod of the head, responded. 'Yeah, the Iditarod and obviously it would have no chance. So, undoubtedly you've been barking up the wrong tree.'

'Touché, but let's look at things' Simon said as he settled himself into his chair in preparation for a prolonged review of events. 'To get himself into the position he found himself, Morton required two people; one to thrust the knife and one to shove him in front of the train, just to make sure the attack was going to be fatal. And yes, we have considered that Rosetta may have been involved in a slight case of mariticide but it might be a bit difficult to pursue any action in that regard as she's dead.'

Gally nodded in acceptance of Simon's appraisal of the circumstances. 'Yes, I'll go along with that,' he said. 'Unfortunately, the state of the body ruled out a thorough examination, despite my efforts to put all the pieces back together. As a consequence, my only irrefutable conclusion is that Morton Blakey was, indeed, done to death and that his condition resulted from the massive trauma to one hundred percent of his body bought about by his unavoidable collision with a metropolitan electric train which is, in itself, a tad unusual.'

'Yeah, those runaway electric trains can be hazardous to your health,' came Noel's dry comment with a snigger.

'Enough of the jokes, Sergeant Elliott,' scolded Simon at Noel's attempt at inappropriate witticism. 'And Gally, have you any thoughts on the matter which aren't contained in the written report. I daresay you must have some views that you can't substantiate with hard scientific evidence?'

Gally folded his arms and, for a few moments, stared at the ceiling. 'Okay. Crime scene investigators failed to find the knife shoved into Blakey's back. In any case, I have my doubts that the stab, made by a left-handed person, would have been fatal as the wound didn't appear to be deep enough to cause any significant damage.'

'How do you know the knifer was left-handed?' Noel asked, somewhat intrigued.

'Presumably both the knifer and the pusher stood behind the victim with the victim facing the tracks. Now, the stab was made to the left-hand side of the lower back...'

'Yeah, okay. But basically, you're saying the knifer was left-handed and an apprentice in the art of stabbing people?' Simon interjected.

'In spades,' Gally replied. 'We've found that most stabbers have a sizeable chip on their shoulder or are just plain angry. A single stab wound would suggest the assailant was not over-whelmed by a sudden fit of anger but instead probably nurtured a long term intense dislike for the victim. And in this particular case, I'd say the knifer was a complete amateur in the art of sticking a knife into someone.'

Noel scratched the back of his head as he considered Gally's perception of one of the unidentified collaborators in the unexpected and unusual passing of Mr Morton Blakey, MP. 'Is there any possibility that Zheng was one of the people to have snuffed out Blakey? Like, it's not as though there was any love lost between Blakey and Zheng, in fact Zheng probably had a pretty good motive to slit Blakey's throat.'

'There's always a possibility, irrespective of how remote that possibility is,' Simon replied. 'If Zheng was a participant in Blakey's murder, it's unlikely Zheng's accomplice would turn around and kill Zheng. That would suggest there's a third party involved, with that third party, whoever it may be, doing away with Zheng.'

'Well, all I know is that Blakey would have found it difficult to kill Zheng as Blakey was already dead. Irrespective of whether Zheng was involved in anyone's murder, I'd say there's at least some unknown third party involved, and we haven't started to look at Rosetta's demise yet,' Noel said with an air of detachment.

Simon heaved a sigh and, with a look not quite of total disinterest, shifted his gaze to Gally who had been sitting quietly listening to the detective's hypothesis. 'Okay, Gally, before we get to Rosetta, do you have any thoughts on Zheng's jugular vein attack?'

Doctor Gallymore pressed his lips together and nodded. 'Yes, there are a few misconceptions that need to be cleared up. First off, Zheng wasn't stabbed in the neck and there wasn't, contrary to popular belief, a knife protruding therefrom. In fact, from my not insignificant experience in such matters, I found the attack on Mr Zheng quite unique. Usually when one attacks the throat of a potential victim with a knife, the person will generally try to slit the throat in what is termed as the "from ear to ear" method. However, this particular attack, carried out with a serrated edge knife, was conducted from behind and directed at the right-hand side of the victim's neck.'

'Yech, nasty. That would really make a mess of the jugular,' Noel commented.

'Yes, but as we have four jugular veins, two on either side of the throat, the killer was sure to mess up at least one of them. But the killer hit the jackpot when he sliced through one of the carotid arteries, the thing that takes the blood from the heart to the brain. Rip that away and exsanguination sets in and you end up dead pretty quickly,' Gally explained to the two attentive detectives.'

'Exsanguination?' Noel enquired.

'Bled to death, or you could say Zheng exsanguinated,' Gally clarified.

'And have you seen this type of attack carried out before?' Simon asked, a little disconcerted at the thought of having his gizzard gutted with a bread knife.

Gally shook his head. 'No, I haven't and have no great desire to see another one; all very messy. I've read where there's evidence of similar attacks having been carried out in some Asian countries, notably Taiwan, China and Hong Kong. Authorities believe it's a hallmark attack by one of the triad sub cultures, but authorities seem reluctant to pursue such offences.'

'Boy, they do play rough,' Simon contended. 'However, I have an idea we need to have a little chat with John Chang, if we can find the man. He's the missing link in all this, and just because he's maintained a low profile doesn't mean we should forget about him. And now we come to Rosetta, although she was dead before Zheng.'

'Whoa, just stop right there,' Galley demanded. 'Before we go any further, there's one thing I haven't mentioned and that's the time-line factor. Both Zheng and Rosetta were done away with on the same night. Obviously I can't be too specific as to the time of death of each of the victims as both had what we would call a somewhat premature departure. However, I would find it a tad ironical if Zheng visited

Rosetta, tossed her overboard and made sure she drowned, drive from Rushcutter Bay to China Town and get himself murdered. Now, that's a pretty busy night for one person.'

'Yes, but we don't know if Zheng did visit Rosetta on the good ship *Lollypop*,' Simon commented.

'*Gemini*' Noel corrected.

'Yeah okay, so let's get on with Rosetta's murder,' Simon said. 'First thing, what has Dave Harris up at The Cross come up with, Noel?'

Noel picked up a folder from his "Pending" tray and extracted a report provided by the crime scene forensic team. The team had poked around the *Gemini* following the recovery of Rosetta's body from Sydney Harbour, a perfectly logical step considering Rosetta had been using Graham's boat as a sanctuary following the spectacular death of her dearly beloved husband, Morton.

'Evidence taken from *Gemini* by the crime scene team has established the presence of one male and two females onboard the boat on the night in question. Accounting for Rosetta, that would mean one male and one female visitor, identification of both unknown, were aboard. Fingerprints were taken but no match recorded which means whoever was onboard hasn't a police record. I suppose it might be an idea to send a copy of the prints to Hong Kong to see if they can come up with anything, although I'd put money on the unidentified female being Jezebel Dawkins,' Noel asserted.

'Oh, and now you're quite finished with the identification of one of the suspects, why is it you think the identification of the female person will turn out to be Jezebel?' Simon asked.

'Okay. There were three women in this little affair that have now been reduced to two. The two existing women are Louisa Lee and Jezebel Dawkins, and I don't think Louisa has any involvement in what's going on. That, by elimination, leaves Jezebel standing out like a shag on a rock,' Noel replied having reached his indisputable and undoubted conclusion.

Simon turned to Gally with raised eyebrows. 'So, Gally, in view of the injuries to Rosetta, presumably made during the drowning process, do you think Jezebel would have been able to wield a boathook around with the dexterity and strength needed to keep Rosetta in the water?'

Gallymore gave a quick "haven't a clue" shrug of the shoulders. 'Not knowing Jezebel, I'm unable to give an opinion. If she has the build and strength of an amazon, probably. If she's more like a dainty, delicate little lady, no. If it was one of the two visitors to the boat on that night who wielded the boathook, I'd say it would have been the male visitor.'

'Oh, that's just great,' Simon remonstrated. 'Means and opportunity but, as far as we know, no-one had a motive. Let's start with Chang. Why in the world would Chang have wanted Rosetta Blakey dead? After all, it would have been Rosetta and Zheng who shared something in common; the mutual loathing of Morton Blakey, notwithstanding that the dislike would have to have been provoked by entirely different reasons.'

Noel threw both arms in the air in exaltation. 'Eureka, and there you have it. It must have been David Zheng and Rosetta Blakey who murdered Morton Blakey whatever their motives were.'

Simon shook his head in despair. 'Yeah, well whoopee duck. And just how do you propose to get a conviction against either one of your enterprising miscreants? While I think you're probably right, and despite zillions of people in close proximity to the killing ground, it's not like we're being inundated with eyewitnesses coming forward to dob in our suspected culprits. And even if there were, it's not like either Rosetta or Mr Zheng is in a position to defend themselves. So Gally, what's your take on Noel's assessment?'

Gally pursed his lips and considered the question. 'Well, anything's possible. If the two were working together, I would say Rosetta did the knifing and Zheng the pushing, if Zheng had been there at all, which I doubt. As I have said, the knife wound was not fatal and was perpetrated by a novice in the art of sticking a knife into someone's back.'

'And you believe the wound inflicted by the knife-sticker consistent with what you would expect if the sticking was carried out by a lady?' suggested Noel.

'Yes, probably, although I'm sure a lady wouldn't be so brazen. But if it wasn't a lady, or a woman, my money would be on a bloke being the stabber, although it might have been two women, or two men,' Gally replied with just a touch of cynicism, 'although I prefer to think a man had to be the pusher. Blakey wasn't a small man and it might've been a bit of a problem for a woman to push him from the platform out in front of the train. The push would have to have been a quick shove and done with a bit of finesse so not to draw attention. And getting back to what I said earlier, the stab was most likely inflicted by a left-handed person and, correct me if I'm wrong, Rosetta was left-handed. And not to put a too finer point on things, Simon, Noel's assessment of the situation has just shot your hypothesis to pieces.'

'Oh, do tell, Doctor Gallymore?' Just where have I blundered?' Simon asked somewhat perplexed.

'You seem to accept Noel's conclusion that Zheng and Rosetta knocked off Morton Blakey and we have the idea that it must have been either Chang, Zheng, Daniel Dawkins, Clyde Fortesque or Jezebel who kept Rosetta in the water until she drowned. While you might be right in regards to Rosetta's involvement in Morton's death, I think we can discount the Premier for no other reason other than he wouldn't want to get his hands dirty, and Zheng because he was over at China Town getting himself murdered.'

Simon frowned as he gathered his thoughts and contemplated the vexing problem. After a pregnant pause in the office discussion as to just who killed who, he pushed his chair back from his desk and gave the armrest of his chair a thump in a show of dogged determination. 'So that leaves us with either John Chang or Daniel Dawkins as the male visitor. Right, there are two people we need to have a little chat with. First off, there's Jezebel Dawkins, who we think was one of visitors to see Rosetta on the *Gemini* the night she was drowned, and the other is John Chang, the good mate of David Zheng, or should I say, the ex good mate of David Zheng.'

Chapter 27

Before opening the door to her office, Jezebel paused and turned to the two detectives. 'Well, gentlemen, I suspect you're here on account of Rosetta's drowning. Terrible thing that, poor girl. Heaven knows, I tried to convince her she should learn to swim, but she was scared witless of things you can find in the water. But before we continue, you'd better come in as I would prefer some privacy,' she said as she ushered the two detectives into a neatly organised office; not quite Henry's, Simon thought after having cast a quick appraising glance around the room.

'I hope we don't need Daniel as he's not feeling too well today and is taking a sickie,' Jezebel announced, forestalling the obvious enquiry.

'No, we've just a few questions you might be able to help us with,' Noel responded as he and Simon seated themselves in front of Jezebel's desk, which was rather unpretentious in comparison to those the detectives had recently come across. 'First off, we're in receipt of reliable information that you and another person visited Rosetta on Graham Lee's boat, the *Gemini*, on the night of the drowning,' Noel lied in a tree shaking exercise. 'You will appreciate that, under the circumstances, the name of the person is vital to our enquiries.'

'Yes, but neither he nor I had anything to do with Rosetta's death. So what. She fell overboard and drowned, big deal. That's just one of the hazards of boating, especially if you can't swim.'

Noel closed his eyes and slowly shook his head in a display of disappointment. My, my, all the sympathy of a parking inspector with a quota to fill, he thought. After a deep sigh he tried again. 'Yes, Mrs Dawkins, we're well aware of the circumstances surrounding the death of Rosetta Blakey. Unfortunately, you seem to be missing the point on a number of factors. To start with, as Rosetta was a non-swimmer, it is doubtful she would have entered the water voluntarily. The only other options available for her to get into the pickle she got herself into would be to fall overboard accidently, be deliberately pushed by someone or she committed some diabolical form of suicide.'

Jezebel sat back and folded her arms. 'Well, I doubt very much if Rosetta would have committed suicide, and if you think I pushed her over the side, you're nuts. I wouldn't have anything like the strength needed to lift her up over the railing and shove her in. And you seem to be forgetting, the boat was parked at the marina so whoever threw her in would have to have coaxed her to the right-hand side of the boat otherwise she would have landed on the jetty.'

'The boat was moored at the marina, and it would have been the starboard side' corrected Noel.

'Moored?' Jezebel questioned.

'Yes. You don't park a boat, you moor it,' Noel clarified.

'Well, who cares?' came Jezebel's swift retort.

Having listened to Noel's attempt to garner some useful information on the death of Rosetta Blakey, Simon entered the verbal stoush. 'Mrs Dawkins, Sergeant Elliott has, quite rightly, asked you for the name of the other person who visited

Rosetta on the particular night she was murdered. As you seem reluctant to divulge this information, we will take it you were involved in the elimination of Rosetta Blakey and our investigation will proceed accordingly.'

'Hey, hang on, who said anything about elimination? I thought Rosetta drowned,' Jezebel said with a touch of disquiet in her voice.

Simon twitched his head sideways and pressed his lips together. 'Yep, she sure did drown, and no-one is disputing that fact. Problem is that whether she could swim or not was totally immaterial to her situation. Someone using a boathook and a little prodding wanted her to stay in the water. Now, as you are reluctant to cooperate in this matter and, as you were present on the *Gemini* the night of her demise, it is not beyond the bounds of possibility you were involved in Rosetta's unfortunate death.'

'Aah, come on, Detective, get real. Rosetta was alive and kicking when I left with John.'

'You mean John Chang?'

'Of course I mean John Chang. Who else?'

Simon leant forward, hand on one hip while the other squeezed the bridge of his nose. 'Okay, Mrs Dawkins, why did you and John Chang go to see Rosetta on the night she drowned?'

Jezebel picked up a pen and started to idly fiddle. 'I'd been speaking to John earlier in the day and mentioned I was thinking of going to see Rosetta that night. Although Daniel and I have our differences, we do agree on many things, but his philandering isn't one of them and he'd been philandering with Rosetta. Unfortunately, his involvement with Rosetta was getting a little too intense for my liking and I wanted to have a quiet word to her. Anyway, John said he would like to talk to Rosetta and explain that there was no animosity as far as he was concerned in what Morton had done. I know that sounds a pretty lame excuse but I wasn't going to question him about it. Irrespective of his real reason for wanting to see Rosetta, we agreed to meet over there and see her together.'

'Now, just stop right there,' exclaimed Noel. 'So, you both drove your own vehicles over to Rushcutter Bay. Why was that, Mrs Dawkins?'

'Simple. John drove his car as he's currently living south of the bridge and I had driven mine because I happen to live on the north side, which was a bit out of his way. Apart from that, I asked him if he wanted a lift and he said no. That was his decision and I wasn't going to question the whys or wherefores.'

'You say Mr Chang is living on the south side of the bridge?' Simon asked, his interest piqued.

'Yes. Would you like me to be a little more specific, DCI Webster?' Jezebel asked with a coy smile.

'It would be appreciated.'

'Unfortunately, DCI Webster, while I might be able to get myself there, I haven't a clue what the address is. Under the circumstances, I regret that I am unable to be more specific,' Jezebel returned with a blatant look of deceit.

'So, Mrs Dawkins, at the moment you've had an involvement with three people who have recently ended up very much dead. There's every indication that you have overlooked this minor fact and have failed to grasp the seriousness of your situation. You claim you had nothing to do with the death of Rosetta and that she was alive and kicking when you left the boat. Well, I'm sorry, but Jack the Ripper would claim he had nothing to do with the five murders he committed. Well, how about Mister Chang. Could he have thrown Rosetta overboard?'

'Hell's bells, Mr Webster. Don't you listen? I haven't killed anyone, and I haven't a clue as to if John Chang threw her in or didn't throw her in. If he did, he would have had to return to the boat as we left at the same time.'

'And when you left, Rosetta was still alive and in the

company of Mr Chang?' Simon asked again in the hope of some contradiction in Jezebel's answer.

'No, DCI Webster, I've already told you, John and I left at the same time and, apart from the effects of a couple of wines, she was sound as a bell.'

'And everything was amicable on your departure?' Simon asked.

'Strangely, yes it was. Although I had gone to see Rosetta with a bee in my bonnet about her fling with my husband, it all turned out quite amicably when she pointed out a few home truths, like my little fling with Morton. We had a few giggles and a few wines and everything ended up hunky-dory. My marriage to Daniel might not be all lovey-dovey, but he's a very wealthy man and I'm not going to surrender him up to anyone, unless the price is right, of course. Yes, initially I might have had a motive for shoving Rosetta overboard but, as I said, I didn't. Sure, Mr Chang might have after I left, but I very much doubt it as I can't see he had a motive for killing her.'

Simon heaved a sigh before considering his next move. 'So, you and John Chang left together and both of you drove your own vehicles directly to your respective premises for the night?'

'We might have left the boat together but we didn't leave Rushcutter Bay together. I'd had a few glasses of wine and realised it might be safer to get a taxi home. John was good enough to walk me from the boat up to Beach Road, the main road in front of the marina, and hail me a cab. I can only presume he then drove home, although he could have returned and heaved Rosetta overboard, or he could have taken a trip to the moon. I haven't a clue what he did.'

For some strange reason, Simon was struck with a sense of fedupness. Crikey, Rosetta's dead, Zheng's dead, Morton's dead. Who cares, he thought. 'Okay, Mrs Dawkins, we'll skip

Rosetta's drowning for the time being. I take it you are aware of the death of David Zheng?'

'Of course,' Jezebel replied. 'Gem Property and Mr Zheng were heavily involved with a proposal to redevelop a site in the city. Mr Zheng was over here quite often to discuss matters with both Daniel and myself. Since his death, John seems to have taken over negotiations. All we're waiting for is for the matter of foreign ownership of the property to be resolved and then we can proceed with the development.'

'Seeing you must have got to know Mr Zheng fairly well, have you any idea who would want to kill him?' Noel asked.

'No, no-one,' Jezebel replied without having to think about it. 'Obviously there has been a number of survey questionnaires conducted throughout the area and all support the plan to build a hotel on the site. Mr Zheng was the overseas negotiator in the deal that will rid Sydney of a seedy gambling casino and replace it with an international six-star hotel, along with the associated employment it will create. The Premier is all for it as he believes the project will generate a lot of money into the state's coffers. No, Sergeant, Mr Zheng was doing us all a favour and our injunction taken out against the current owner of the property is providing us the opportunity to facilitate all mandatory prerequisites for the demolition in preparation for construction to commence.'

'That would suggest all the bureaucratic necessities, such as building codes, environmental considerations, planning authority conditions and a host of other bureaucratic nonsense, quite apart from the sale of the property, have all been taken care of?' Noel asked, somewhat surprised that Gem was so far advanced with proceedings.

Jezebel shrugged. 'Well, irrespective of what other people might think, the redevelopment of the Taipan Club is a fait accompli. The overseas investors, for whom Mr Zheng was acting, are determined to establish a foothold in the hotel industry here in Sydney. With what appears to be unlimited finance, and the support of our own government, okay, the Premier's support, Graham Lee's stupid idea of some ridiculous residential scheme has as much chance as a snowball in hell.'

'Well, I don't think either Graham or Henry Haynes think it's game over,' Simon said, somewhat annoyed at Jezebel's smugness.

Jezebel pushed her chair back from her table and started to rock slowly back and forward exuding an air of confidence. 'Now, if you're talking about Morton Blakey's murder, that's a whole new ball game,' she said, effectively changing the topic of discussion. The only two people I can think of who he might have had a motive to kill Morton would have been David Zheng and Rosetta. As it is, I'd say it would be quite difficult for any prosecutor to get a conviction against either one of them. Come to think of it, can you get a conviction against someone in absentia, like when they're already dead?'

Simon's face contorted in deep deliberation before he addressed the question. 'Well, I for one would hope that if the person on trial were to be deceased, that person's presence in court, who wouldn't really be a person having adopted the role of a cadaver, or a corpse, would pay the court the courtesy of being as far away as possible from the judicial proceedings, especially in the summer time. Crikey, I wonder how a corpse would react to a prosecution's intense cross-examination. Anyway, what would you do, Jezebel? Get the corpse to sit on the stand and ask it how it pleads. In short, the answer to your question is yes and no, as it all depends on a number of factors, although in Zheng's case I would say no. In fact, I doubt the judge would let the trial go ahead. As it is, we don't know if Zheng did kill Morton so the question is purely academic.'

Jezebel harrumphed in disgust. 'As far as Rosetta is concerned, Morton's death would have suited her down to the ground, irrespective of who the killer was. It's just unfortunate she won't be in a position to benefit by his sudden demise due to her own unexpected departure from planet Earth, unless, of course, she managed to cast him adrift first. Anyway, we reap what we sow and as Rosetta has already rid herself of a couple of husbands, maybe the worm turned and it was time for her to go.'

'Hey, now just back up a tick. I thought you and Rosetta were mates and you're now saying she's a serial killer who's murdered both her husbands?' Noel, somewhat surprised by the revelation, inquired.

'I suppose you spoke to Rosetta following Morton's death. Whatever impression she made on you is probably a sham, and no, we're not mates but we tolerate each other. After all, my husband was shagging Rosetta while Morton and I were at it; sort of unofficial swappies. Anyway, Rosetta was an inveterate liar and couldn't lie straight in bed. Provided you took everything she said with a grain of salt, you might end up closer to the truth. And no, I don't know that she actually did murder Alvin or Morton, although there's always the possibility she did both of the in.'

Jezebel gave a sigh as she ran her fingers through her long black hair. 'But isn't it just ducky. Rosetta wanted hubby dead for personal reasons and Zheng wanted him dead in revenge for stuffing up the Premier's bill and his subsequent takeover of the Taipan Club. Now surely, Detective Chief Inspector Webster, it can't be all that difficult to work out just who did kill Morton Blakey.'

Chapter 28

'Maybe she's right,' Noel speculated as he fashioned a piece of paper into a jet fighter aircraft. 'Although the police on duty at Town Hall Station took statements of those people leaving the platform, none were taken from those who chose to wait around and get on the train they intended to get on in the first place.'

'You mean the killer train?' Simon inquired.

'Yep, the killer train. And with no CCTV of the platform, or anywhere else in the station, thanks to all those whacko civil libertarians, Jack the Ripper or the seven dwarfs could have done the deed. Irrespective of who we might think is, or are, the killers, it's going to be difficult to place any suspect at the scene of the crime. That leaves us with one out of three.'

'One out of three?' Simon enquired.

'Motive. With so many people on the platform we could pick any two out of the zillions having both the means and opportunity. However, it might be a tad difficult to find two commuters with a motive to kill Blakey, which there obviously were. We've already established there was no love lost between Rosetta and her husband. It's possible she might have had a rethink after the kidnap fiasco and decided to go for broke and take everything of hubby's estate by shunting him onto the tracks. And we know Zheng had good grounds for assisting Rosetta get rid of Morton out of sheer revenge,' Noel reasoned as he jettisoned his paper F104 into the air with the same result as many of the real widowmakers.

Simon pressed his lips together and stared at nothing in particular for a moment. 'So, we have one victim and two murderers, both with totally different motives for doing away with Mr Blakey.'

'Yeah, but that's making the assumption our killers were Rosetta and Zheng. What if they weren't?' Noel queried.

'We're back to square one. And no doubt Detective Superintendent Nigel Fisher would take on the mantle as the prickliest cactus in the desert, and you know what that would mean,' Simon said with more than a hint of trepidation.

Noel pulled his chair closer to his desk and, with a closed fist, thumped the desk with a resounding thud. 'Okay, boss, let's get the hell out of here and go find whatsis name.'

'I take it you mean John Chang?' Simon said as he grabbed his coat and headed for the door before Noel was out of his chair.

'Well, yes I did. And I suppose I can take it you approve of my suggestion?'

'Yes to the getting the hell out of here bit, before Fisher can get his teeth into us. And we may as well try and find this Hong Kong high flyer as we do need some answers.'

'SO, just where do you propose to start looking for our elusive John Chang?' Noel asked as he piloted the unmarked police car down George Street heading for The Rocks. 'I asked Immigration if they had an address but they were unable to help.'

'And why doesn't that surprise me?' Simon scoffed. 'The

thing is, if Chang has taken over negotiations following Zheng's death, I bet both Gem Development and the Premier know exactly where to contact Chang.'

'So?'

'Yeah, okay, I know what that means. But I don't relish the idea of confronting Fortesque again. Talk about vanity; he's as vain as Varicus.'

'Oh yeah, and who's Varicus?' Noel asked in total ignorance of the little foibles of the human body.

'He was the Greek God of sore legs and was known as Varicus Vain,' Simon answered with all serious intent, but with a smirk. 'Still, that doesn't detract from the fact that the Premier really is a pretentious prat and an unsavoury character, and that's over and above what you'd expect from the general run-of-the-mill politician. Anyway, does this place ring a bell?' Simon asked in a more buoyant tone as Noel miraculously found a parking spot in Argyle Street.

Noel gazed out the window at the old dark brown brick building where he and Simon had started the policing careers. 'Cripes, a million years ago and a lot of water under the bridge,' he said with a smile. 'And there's the pub across the road where Benny and Jacko were trying to do a heist and you and Sergeant Rose busted 'em. Still, it's good to see they're still able to keep themselves out of the slammer, probably more by good luck than good management.'

The two detectives, having found a sidewalk coffee shop, placed their order, found a table and took time out to sit and relax for a moment in the morning sunshine. With a giant cruise liner having recently berthed no more than a hundred metres away at Circular Quay and, with The Rocks being a historic part of the city, many of the seafaring tourists would soon be exploring the old buildings, ruins and laneways of the colony's first settlement.

'Okay, boss, I'll make a deal,' Noel said as he placed his empty cup on the saucer. 'I'll go and have a talk with Daniel

Dawkins while you go and have a quiet verbal with the Premier.'

'Gee whiz, Noel,' Simon exclaimed, 'here I was enjoying a quiet brew and a bit of sunshine and you have to stuff it up by bringing work into it. But okay, although I think you have the better end of the deal.'

Noel shrugged and gave Simon a look of mock pity. 'Gee, boss, rank does have its privileges which means you get to see the head honcho. But seeing I'll be chatting to Danny D, is there anything specific you want me to ask, apart from where this Johnny Chang can be found?'

'No, not really. Everything seems to have stalled at the moment and even Graham Lee can't do anything with that preventative injunction in place. While not wishing to appear too pessimistic, I'm beginning to think these murders were a complete waste of time, at least to the murdering sods who carried them out, and everything will revert back to where it was before the killings started. You can drop me off up at Macquarie Street then you can skip over the bridge to North Sydney. I'll meet you back at Day Street.'

Chapter 29

'So, how'd you get on with Daniel Dawkins?' Simon asked before Noel had time to remove his coat.

'I didn't. Both Jezebel and Danny boy weren't at work today and, according to the receptionist, they haven't been to work for the last couple of days.' Having arranged his coat on the hat stand, Noel sat at his desk, notebook in hand. 'Apparently Mr Dawkins hasn't been feeling too well lately and has been taking some time off. It's only recently that Jezebel has chosen to spend some time at home to look after him while continuing to negotiate with John Chang. And no, the receptionist hasn't a clue as to where he hangs out. How about you? I've no doubt the Premier was a ball of sociability and only too willing to prove he's the font of all knowledge. And as knowledge is power, he's the sort of bloke who wants to let everyone know how powerful he is, provided you're conversant with the politician's dialect and can understand what he's talking about.'

'Crikey, Noel, I never thought of it that way, but I know what you mean. You hear a politician being interviewed on TV and, after a spiel in response to a question, you never know if the polly has answered the question or not. Seems they all have the ability to prattle on and say nothing. Anyway, he says he doesn't know where to contact Mr Chang as Chang will contact him once the overseas bill and injunction things have been resolved. Once those issues have been sorted out, they will make a move on the Taipan Club. And if you think I believe Mr Fortesque doesn't know where Chang is, you must think I think pigs really can fly. Maybe the head honcho needs a dose of sodium pentothal to loosen his brain.'

'So, Fortesque is happy the way things are going?' Noel asked as he pushed his chair back and rested his legs on the desk.

'Oh, I'd say he's over the moon,' Simon replied. 'I had a word with Jackie on the way out which only went to prove if you want answers to questions, don't ask the boss. She really was a breath of fresh air after talking to Fortesque. According to her, the Premier and Lorraine, you know, the lovely red haired very personal assistant, they're off on another fact-finding mission, this time to Iceland to see how they generate thermal electricity forgetting, of course, they could do the same thing in New Zealand.'

Noel pulled a scornful look and raised his eyes to the ceiling. 'Well, whoopee duck. Mr Chang must have made another instalment on the quid pro quo arrangement. I suppose the injunction taken out against Graham Lee doesn't stop Gem from going about their business and no doubt the Premier is making sure all the boxes are ticked for a government takeover of the club and subsequent sale to Chang's mob. The amount of compensation paid to Graham will be nickels and dimes, and the government will sell it off to this overseas mob for not much more, the big bikkies going to the politicians involved.'

'Well, they can't, at least I don't think they can,' Simon said doubtfully. 'I'm no legal expert but I read somewhere where it says the government can't on-sell a property to a developer. But I s'pose in this case they wouldn't be, they'd be on-selling it to an overseas financial conglomerate with a property developer lined up to do their bidding. The whole thing would certainly make the Premier look a bit sus if anyone found out the extent of the shonky being perpetrated. The trouble for us is that I doubt there isn't much he wouldn't do, including the occasional murder, to make sure no-one outside those involved becomes aware of what's going on.'

'I don't know, but I wouldn't put it passed John Chang to have a few notches on his six-gun seeing he's got something to do with a triad gang,' Noel suggested.

'Oh, yes, talking of Chang. One thing Jackie did give me was an address. Chang wrote it down in the visitor register which seems a bit dumb if he wanted it to remain unknown. Anyway, it seems he's shacked up in an apartment down at The Rocks, not far from where we were yesterday.'

'So, what's keeping us? Shouldn't we be scurrying off to nab the bloke?' Noel said, a little surprised at the apparent lack of urgency to interview Mr Chang.'

Simon, his elbow on the chair's armrest, held his chin while he reflected on the sense of pessimism from which he had been overtaken. Shaken from his reverie, he considered Noel's uncomplicated questions. 'To put it bluntly, Noel, I'm more concerned with the welfare of Daniel Dawkins. Something doesn't ring true and I smell a rat; a dead one. Danny's a strapping young man in the prime of life. Trouble is, he didn't look the picture of health over at Manly and now he's taking more than the odd sickie which leads me to believe he's on a downhill spiral. If we scurry off anywhere, it should be over to wherever he and Jezebel live just to make sure he is.'

'Sure he is what?' Noel enquired, not quite up to speed with Simon's thinking.

'Alive.'

Noel twitched backwards on his chair, the hideous significance of Simon's inferred notion coming somewhat unexpectedly. 'Hey, hang about. Whatever gives you the idea old Danny boy is a bit off key?'

'To me Mr Dawkins doesn't look a well man and seems to be getting a lot worse. He has that nasty looking bruise on his leg and, although I'm no Doc Gallymore, such bruising can be symptomatic of arsenic poisoning. Obviously, Jezebel has plenty of opportunity to administer small doses of whatever it is she might be administering over a period of time. What we do know is that their relationship ain't a bed of roses, but whether it's bad enough for her to do away with Daniel is another thing.'

'But why?' Noel exclaimed, somewhat mystified by Simon's latest notion. 'She did say she wouldn't give Daniel up to anyone, unless it was worth her while.'

'Yeah well, since Louisa had a brief chat to Rosetta about making life uncomfortable for Morton, and no doubt Jezebel listened in on the conversation, both Morton and Rosetta have shoved off planet Earth. Okay, so it's a long shot but maybe, just maybe, Jezebel might have decided to get in on a bit of matricide and started to feed Daniel a dose of arsenic with his dinner. After all, it's not like he's short a quid and, as you just said, Jezebel did mention that it would have to be to her financial benefit to let him off the matrimonial hook. Maybe she believes Gem could be more profitable with a woman at the helm, and she expects to be that woman.'

Noel shook his head in wonder. 'And you think that, irrespective of whether Daniel wants to be cast adrift or not, Jezebel might have decided it's time for him to go. And from what you say, it sounds like you think Rosetta did take part in Morton's death.'

'Well, she wasn't backward in coming forward in expounding her undying love for Morton, or lack thereof, and you have to admit, it is a possibility we haven't given serious consideration to. Maybe Graham's plan for the Taipan Club started the ball rolling down a very long and slippery slope,' Simon said and gave a "perhaps" sort of shrug. 'And did you find out anything on Rosetta's phone calls while over at Crows Nest?'

'Nothing unexpected. Seems she was pretty talkative with both Louisa and Jezebel, but a woman can be talkative to a brick wall,' Noel replied.

'So, it's not as though she was calling Jack the Ripper to get in on the act,' Simon pronounced as he leaned back on his chair and clasped his hands behind his head. 'Anyway, maybe we should go over to wherever and look in on Daniel. He might be okay, but then again, he might be dead.'

Noel harrumphed. 'So, we go over to wherever, knock on the door and whoever opens it, we just ask to see the dead or alive Daniel. Sounds a bit like Schrodinger's cat to me; Daniel's both alive and dead until we see for ourselves whether he is or isn't. I still think we'll end up looking like two real gits if there's nothing wrong with him.'

Conceding the possibility, Simon continued. 'Yeah, well, if he's dead I think Jezebel will have a few questions to answer.'

Chapter 30

'Geeze boss, whoever said he wasn't short of a quid got that one right,' Noel remarked as the two detectives made their way to the front door of the imposing mansion that over-looked the placid waters of Middle Harbour and the golden sands of Balmoral Beach.

'Yeah, maybe there's something in the saying, the rich get richer and the poor get poorer and, unfortunately, I can't see me graduating from the latter to the former,' Simon said ruefully as he pressed the ornate doorbell with an extended index finger. 'You did check to see if the Dawkins were at work today?'

'Sure did. I spoke to the receptionist who said Jezebel had dropped in early this morning and said she would be out for discussions with Mr Chang for the rest of the day. Apparently, Daniel wouldn't be in at all as he was spending the day at home, because he's sick, or so she said.'

There being little in the way of a response to Simon's initial finger pressing exercise, he attacked the doorbell again, this time with an aggravated, impatient fervency. With every indication his latest announcement of a visitor presence on the doorstep would prove as unsuccessful as his initial bell ringing exercise, Simon tried the door handle and, surprisingly, found it to be unlocked. 'Okay Noel, if we go inside, we're breaking the law. But, if we go inside and find Daniel dead, we could always say we believed there was a health hazard, or at least a health and safety concern present, and Daniel was the subject of that concern.'

Noel grimaced. 'Yeah, that's all well and good, but if he's dead he'd no longer be a health and safety consideration, at least not until he started to decompose. Then he might be a health risk, unless someone's taken the time to pop him in the refrigerator.'

'Well, in for a penny, in for a pound,' Simon declared and pushed the door open. 'Seeing he's supposed to be sick, we'll check the bedrooms first, and they're going to be upstairs, so let's get to it.'

Before the detectives could commence their search for the bedrooms and a possible Daniel Dawkins, their attention was drawn to the sound of drinking glasses clinking together and a sudden muffled "thump". 'Where'd that come from?' Simon appealed with a touch of desperation in his voice.

'This one here, I think,' came Noel's reply as he headed for a door leading from a long hallway.

On entering the room, neither Simon nor Noel could discern anything of significance, or anything else for that matter, as the drawn heavy drapes darkened the room sufficiently to impede normal vision. To overcome this initial impediment to proceedings, Noel used his initiative and flicked on the light switch located next to the door to reveal…

'Crikey, the poor bugger's fallen out of bed,' Noel blurted.

'Yes, I can see that, and looks like he took his bedside apothecary with him,' Simon declared, referring to the scattered bottles of pills, a water jug and a drinking glass on the floor.

'Is he dead?' Noel asked.

'No, not yet. Come and give us a hand and get him back

into bed. It's better to be dead in bed than to cark in the dark; someone might trip over him, poor bloke.'

It was on completion of this little task that Daniel Dawkins, now comfortably resting in a bedroom that was obviously not the master bedroom, deigned to offer up a word of gratitude to the two detectives, albeit with some difficulty. 'Thanks, fellas,' he wheezed, 'I don't think I would have had the strength to crawl back to bed. But now you're here, and as I seem to be about to kick the bucket, there's a few things I'd like to get off my chest.'

'Whoa, just hold your horses. There's something we should get straight before you go getting anything off your chest,' Noel demanded. 'First things first. Apparently you are in no condition to be able to recognise Detective Chief Inspector Simon Webster and Detective Sergeant Noel Elliott, who we are. As a consequence, I can assure you we are not members of the first estate and certainly not qualified to bear witness to whatever it is you want to expunge from your conscience. Secondly, as we are members of the police force, we came out to Balmoral to see if you were alive or dead as we suspected there was every chance you would have to be one or the other. Now, do we understand each other, Mr Dawkins?'

'Indutably,' Daniel Dawkins mumbled as some dribble seeped from the corner of his mouth.

'I guess he's trying to say "indubitably"', Simon murmured. 'Must say, he doesn't look at all well. What do you think, Noel, should we get him an ambulance, maybe a doctor or something?'

Noel shook his head. 'Well, he is alive. As you're the boss, and if you think he's okay where he is, maybe we should take the opportunity to listen to what he has to say. We can always drive him over to the hospital later ourselves where they'll probably flush him out, if he doesn't die in the meantime.'

Simon nodded and pulled up a chair next to the bed. 'Okay Daniel, what is it you would like to get off your chest?'

Daniel wheezed a piteous deep breath and, with great effort, started his sordid tale. Although having grave difficulty in his articulation, the two detectives were able to determine that Jezebel was in the process of poisoning him, apparently for a number of reasons, not the least his carrying on with Rosetta Blakey. Convinced that the only way he would ever leave the Balmoral mansion would be in a wooden box, Daniel was able to convey to the detectives his fervent desire to make a dying declaration naming Jezebel as his murderer.

'Now, don't you think that might be taking things to the extreme?' Simon asked as his face reflected the unpalatable consequences. 'There's an old proverb that says "The noblest vengeance is to forgive." But you don't think you're noble enough to forgive Jezebel for murdering you?'

'It doesn't matter how noble you are once you're dead,' came Daniel's gurgled response.

Noel, standing at the foot of the bed, scratched his head. 'Yeah, but your dying declaration ain't worth a pinch of salt unless you're dead. Now, as I see it, you can make a declaration to the boss and myself and we'll do nothing to stop you from pegging out. We'll just sit here and watch you die and then take the appropriate action against Jezebel. On the other hand, you can decide you don't want to make a dying declaration and would prefer to go on living. If that is the case, we'll call an ambulance. But as I said, for your declaration to be accepted in court you'll have to be dead. And then again, we can't guarantee Jezebel would be convicted of your murder, and even if she was, she'd probably get a suspended sentence or six months. However, the choice is yours.'

Daniel closed his eyes and slowly shook his head. 'Cripes, you don't give a bloke much of an option. Here I stand to make buckets of money with redeveloping the Taipan Club site and the bloody wife wants to muscle in on the act and take everything I have, including my life, plus all the money the Chinese mob is willing to pay me for their new hotel.'

'Do you know where Jezebel is right now, Daniel?' Simon asked offhandedly.

'Wouldn't have a clue. At work I s'pose. Why, where is she?'

'We have reason to believe she's currently in private discussions with a Mister John Chang whom we believe you have held previous negotiations relating to the Taipan Club redevelopment scheme.'

As Daniel was physically incapable of a fit of rage, he stoically suffered the torment of a dreaded attack of apoplexy in a silence broken only by his guttural struggle for life-giving air. After what would have amounted to a few short moments for Simon and Noel, or a period approaching an eternity of harrowing distress for Daniel, he was able to gain control of his faculties with a newfound vengeance. 'That rotten little... Jezebel!! I knew she wouldn't be able to keep her mitts off that Chang bloke. So, what if he looks like David Carradine and has lots of money. Who cares?'

'So, who's David Carradine when he's at home,' Noel asked, somewhat perplexed having never heard the name before.

Daniel gave an uncomplimentary sneer. 'Holy hell, don't you blokes ever watch good, decent TV. I s'pose you've never heard of Kung Fu, or Grasshopper either. But let's get down to business. You know, well, maybe you don't, but it was Jezebel and Zheng who knocked off Rosetta's husband, that brainless politician Morton Blakey.'

The accusation seemed to have little effect on Simon who remained sitting passively next to the bed. 'Oh, and you can back that up with a little evidence?'

'Yes, of course. I heard Jezebel talking on the phone to Rosetta. Jezebel was miffed with Morton for giving her the flick and Zheng was peeved with him for making life difficult.

Rosetta wanted Morton dead for a number of reasons, although I don't think there was much love lost on either side, and you can bet she let Jezebel know of her loathing of hubby.'

Simon pursed his lips, raised his eyebrows and gave Noel a "what do you think" look. 'Sounds like a lot of hearsay evidence to me,' Noel offered, 'and with Rosetta dead there's only Jezebel who can confirm, or refute, what Daniel has said. Sure, Alf said Rosetta was always on the phone to someone and that someone turned out to be Jezebel. But maybe they were talking about the weather, and I bet my booties Jezebel would never stand up in court and tell everyone they had spoken about knocking somebody off.'

'Aah, crikey, Noel, you've brought up hearsay evidence and now the rule of self-incrimination. Unfortunately I haven't watched enough TV court room dramas to be able to follow all that legal procedure stuff, so maybe we should go and interrupt Jezebel's little tryst with Grasshopper.'

Chapter 31

The apartment cum hotel building was a sky-scraper with many of its rooms and self-contained units providing extensive views of Sydney Harbour, if you could afford the rental, which didn't come cheap. But then again, John Chang had lots of money and could, although just whose money was a moot point and could be open to speculation.

After making the necessary enquiries at the reception counter, Noel dared to ask Simon the question which was either stupidity in the extreme, or a total waste of time. 'He's in apartment number 2502 which happens to be on the twenty fifth floor. Do you want to take the stairs or the elevator?'

Choosing to either ignore the question or feigning deafness, Simon headed for the lifts and pressed the "Up" button. 'So, Noel, seeing our Mr Chang was Mr Zheng's shadow, do you think he'll confirm Daniel's accusation that Zheng and Jezebel killed Morton?'

'I'd say he probably could if he wanted to, but I reckon he probably won't,' Noel replied as the two detectives entered the elevator. 'Problem is that if he does provide confirmation, he'll automatically convict himself of being an accessory, probably both before and after the fact. Chang's no dill so I think the chances of him doing that are as slim as Buckley's.'

'Good thinkin', Noel. But Chang and Jezebel make for strange bed-fellows, if they are involved,' Simon said as he stepped from the elevator after Noel. 'In any event, the next few minutes are sure to be interesting, in more ways than one.'

Noel pressed the door buzzer to room 2502 and, after a few moments, noticed the slight movement behind the door peephole. 'At least someone's home', he said allaying any fears their trip was in vain. A period of silence ensued before both detectives recognised the unmistakable sound of the security chain being either latched or unlatched. Despite the seemingly lack of enthusiasm to welcome the unannounced visitors, the door was finally opened to reveal a suave looking Asian gentleman, albeit a tad taller to what may have been expected, his neatly arranged long black hair matched by his penetrating black eyes. Although dressed in very casual clothing of shorts and T-shirt, and sporting bare feet, Mr Chang oozed sophistication and refinement, a fact that prompted Noel to recall Daniel Dawkins's belief that Jezebel wouldn't be able to keep her mitts off the man.

'Mr Chang?' Simon asked expectantly. 'Mr John Chang?'

'Yes, and you are?'

'I'm Detective Chief Inspector Simon Webster and this is Detective Sergeant Noel Elliott. Do you mind if we come in, or would you prefer to have a little chat standing here in the doorway?'

'Well, Mr Webster, I would prefer not to have a chat with you in the doorway, or anywhere else for that matter, and especially not at the moment as I'm quite busy.'

'Who is it, sweetie?' came the melodious tone of a woman's voice from what was perceived by the detectives as the bedroom.

'Don't tell me,' Simon directed as he screwed his face into a look of intense satirical concentration. 'No, don't tell me, it's on the tip of my tongue. Crikey, I know that voice and it has to belong to Jezebel Dawkins. It's all right, Jezebel, everything's okay. It's DCI Webster and DS Elliott. We'd very much like to have a few words with Mr Chang, but if you're not too busy, we'll take the opportunity to kill two birds with one stone, if you'll excuse the pun, and have a chat with you at the same time,' he said in a raised voice to the unseen Jezebel. 'Now, Mr Chang, I would strongly suggest you invite us in or we can take alternate measures and haul both you and Jezebel down to the nick for a formal interview.'

'If that's the case, you'd better come in,' Mr Chang finally decided. By this time the lovely Jezebel was standing in the centre of the apartment's living room, her arms folded in a somewhat confrontational manner. Noel, after casting a swift and subtle glance in Jezebel's direction, had already come to the unsettling conclusion that the silk robe was the sum total of clothing she was wearing; my, my, I can't imagine what they were up to. Whatever it was, I have grave doubts it was on the agenda for discussion, he thought as he reflected back on the advice given by the Gem receptionist.

After seating themselves in the lavishly decorated sitting room, Simon initiated proceedings by turning to Jezebel. 'Jezebel, we are aware that you and Morton Blakey were involved in a relationship while you were his campaign manager. That relationship appears to have ended some time ago in what we are led to believe were somewhat acrimonious circumstances. Can you tell us whether these circumstances were sufficiently acrimonious for you to be involved in his murder?'

Jezebel turned to Mr Chang, her eyes wide in astonishment, not because of the question itself, but the fact the question, having been asked, her response was expected. 'You've got to be joking. I'm sure if you had any evidence of my involvement in his murder you would never ask such a stupid question but, as you expect an answer, I'll say no, there wasn't. Now, you prove otherwise.'

Wishing to placate the situation, Simon raised his hands in submission and slowly shook his head. 'I apologise for my questioning technique, Jezebel, but we have it on good authority you and David Zheng, may he rest in peace, murdered Mr Blakey, who will probably rest in pieces, thanks to the nature of his death.'

'I think you may be fifty percent correct, Mr Webster,' broke in Mr Chang. Mr Zheng fulfils the motive, means and opportunity requirements of a murder investigation and, as I am sure you have already been appraised of the motive, or at least worked it out for yourself, you'll agree he ticks all the boxes needed to get a conviction.'

'Yes,' interjected Noel, 'but we have already discussed the problems involved in trying to get a conviction against Mr Zheng, not the least being the fact that he's dead.'

'Yes, terrible tragedy that,' Mr Chang replied. 'Have you any idea as to who the murderer of Mr Zheng might be, DCI Webster?'

Simon pressed his lips together and nodded. 'We have a couple of suspects currently under investigation and we expect to make an arrest in the foreseeable future.'

'And what about the politician's wife; what was her name, Lambretta?' Mr Chang asked with just a hint of derision.

'Rosetta, you know, the lady who just happened to get herself murdered on the one night you and Jezebel chose to pay her a visit,' clarified Noel indignantly. Yep, Simon thought, come up here for a nice quiet chat and this bloke turns out to be as useless as an outside dunny on a submarine.

'Getting back to your question, Mr Chang. All I can say is that Rosetta's murder, along with that of Morton Blakey and David Zheng are under investigation, as Jezebel is fully aware,' Simon replied as calmly as his rising blood pressure would allow. 'Just one point we'd like to clarify. At what time did you put Jezebel in a taxi and send her home?'

'I didn't. We both drove our own cars over to Rushcutter Bay and met over there. At the end of the evening, we both left at the same time and drove home. At least I did and I was under the impression that's what Jezebel did.'

'So, as Rosetta was still alive and kicking at the time of your departure, do you have any information you would like to divulge regarding who the perpetrator of her untimely death might be?'

John Chang's face broke into a broad grin. 'Well, this is a turn-up for the books. I may or may not have information that you may or may not have already. Unless you can be a bit more specific on what you know and what you don't know, DCI Webster, anything I might be able to say on the matter may be a total waste of time as you may already be cognizant of the information I may be able to contribute. So, DCI Webster, might I suggest you tell me what you don't know and I'll try to fill in the gaps with information you probably are not acquainted with.'

Simon frowned. 'Yes, I'm well aware my request for any information on the murder of Morton Blakey, Rosetta Blakey and David Zheng may have sounded like a fishing trip, and maybe you're right on that score, it probably was. The point is that although there are three dead bodies at the moment, we now have Daniel Dawkins trying his best to increase that body count. He's of the firm belief his deteriorating health is directly attributed to your actions, Jezebel, and I must say the way he looks I'd say he's well on the way to becoming number four for Doc Gallymore.'

'And how do you work that out?' Jezebel objected angrily. 'Daniel's suffering from a mild case of food poisoning which is a long way from suffering a dose of strychnine or being thrown in front of a train.'

'But the bruise on his leg might be considered as being one

of the symptoms consistent with having been fed a dose of arsenic, as he claims to have been. That, and his current state of health, would suggest he's not in the pink of good health,' Noel said in an effort to appear well versed in the use of toxicants and their mortal effects on humans.

'Oh, for the love of God, Sergeant Elliott. The bruise on his leg was caused when he fell up the stairs on his way to the bedroom. Yes, up the bloody stairs, unfortunately. He hit his leg on the next step up which caused him to bleat and moan like a stuck pig. And if on the off-chance I was going to poison Daniel, which I'm not and haven't already, I would have used antimony for no other reason that I saw it used on a TV murder mystery and it proved very successful.'

'Unfortunately, Mrs Dawkins, your husband is under the impression you are poisoning him,' Noel offered. 'He further believes you and David Zheng killed Morton Blakey.'

Jezebel rose from her chair and walked to the floor to ceiling window where she stood, arms akimbo, and surveyed the panoramic harbour view from the bridge to the distant harbour headlands. Without turning, she addressed the detectives; she didn't care which one in particular as long as someone was listening. 'If Daniel thinks that, I'd say he's delusional and suffering from something far more serious than a bout of food poisoning.

'Let's just suppose, hypothetically, that David Zheng and I did murder Blakey,' Jezebel continued. 'From what I have read in the newspapers, Blakey was stabbed in the back before being thrown in front of the train. I'm sure that if one of the ninety three zillion people on the platform at the time of the killing had come forward to identify the perpetrators of the deed, you would have the perpetrators locked up behind bars. As neither I, nor David Zheng are locked up behind bars, I would consider that some sort of an admission which leads me to believe you haven't a clue as to who the murderers are.'

After jotting a few essential elements of the investigation in his note-book, Simon nodded in reluctant agreement. 'Yes, unfortunately I have to agree with you, up to a point, Jezebel. David Zheng had a clear and definitive motive for killing Morton and would probably be behind bars now except for one minor point; he's dead. On the other hand, we can only speculate as to your motive for doing away with Morton. To clarify the matter, can you give us a good reason why you would want to kill Morton Blakey? And please, don't get me wrong. We're not saying you did help kill Morton, we're just trying to establish if you had sufficient motive to do so if you felt inclined.'

'DCI Webster, you're the policeman and, while I maintain a high regard for the force, I feel there is something incongruous with your method of investigation. You're asking me to provide you with reasons why I would want to murder a person who has just been murdered. I'm sure you don't really expect me to provide you with information that might turn out to be incriminating, even if I were in a position to do so.'

'Aah, come on, Jezebel. You think it's easy to be a cop,' Simon appealed. 'You have no idea just how difficult it is. Even if we knew who the murderer was, that's just the beginning. All the legal stuff we have go through to make sure it's all admissible, relevant and legal. And then there's the paperwork; you wouldn't believe how many reams of paper it takes to get someone to trial. And, to top it off, if we do manage to get it all together, the presiding judge invariably decides that a custodial sentence for a person as deranged as someone of the Jack the Ripper ilk is too inhumane and draconian and that periodic detention and counselling a far more positive solution to the rehabilitation of the offender.'

Simon's little exhibition of verbal paroxysm elicited two very differing, and understandable, reactions. Both Mr Chang and Jezebel, having shared a speechless conversation, the gist of which having been transmitted by nothing more than eye contact and facial expression, chose to remain silent in expectation of further developments. Noel, on the other hand, sat in stunned silence as he tried to decide if Simon was using some ploy to further the investigation. Having decided he wasn't, and that Simon had undergone some sort of mental atrophy, he was hard pressed on what he was supposed to do. After all, the situation Noel found himself had not been covered at the Academy and was not included in any of the manuals.

It was John Chang who broke the silence. 'I apologise in advance for my next question, DCI Webster, but are you feeling all right, headache maybe?'

'What do you mean, am I feeling all right? Does it look like I'm sick or something? So far, we have three cadavers, two on slabs in the morgue and one they're trying to put the pieces back together. On top of that, Daniel Dawkins believes he's knockin' on heaven's door as his darlin' wife feeds him a diet of antimony or arsenic, or something that's not conducive to good health. Now, I ask you, wouldn't you get a bit stroppy if you're trying to do your job only to be confronted by two recalcitrant dipsticks who have their hearts set on making life difficult for you.'

'Now, just hang on to your horses, DCI Webster, there's no need to get personal,' Chang said indignantly. 'Jezebel and I would be only too happy to answer your questions as long as our answers don't put a noose around our neck. You're the policeman and it's your job to find the perpetrators of these foul deeds, not expect the perpetrators to do the job for you.'

'And are you the perpetrators?' Noel asked having crawled his way out of a state of mortification.

Jezebel abruptly turned from the window, arms folded across her chest. 'Look, Sergeant Elliott, either you're as deaf as a lamp post or just plain ignorant. If John and I happen to be the homicidal maniacs you're looking for, it's up to you to come up with the evidence to prove it. Even if we admit to killing Rosetta's husband, which we don't and won't as we didn't, there's not much you can do about it as there's an appalling lack of evidence. I could say the same thing with regards to the deaths of both Rosetta and Mr Zheng. You ain't got nothin' on us, copper, so shove off and leave us alone until you can prove your case.'

Cripes, Bonny and Clyde alive and kicking, Simon thought.

Chapter 32

It was an awkward atmosphere that dominated the detectives return to Day Street, the silence within the police car doing nothing to mitigate the tension between the two men. Noel was unable to recall having ever experienced a falling out with Simon and his little outburst, contrary to expectations, had left him desolate and wondering what the future might hold. Simon was not just his boss; he had been, and hopefully still was, his closest friend, a friendship borne initially out of a professional bond that had developed socially to include the respective wives.

On arrival back at their Day Street office, the situation to an outsider would have appeared quite comical with Detective Chief Inspector Simon Webster sitting at one end of the office and Detective Sergeant Noel Elliott sitting at the other. Obviously not by design but more likely by accident, both detectives had adopted the same seating posture with their arms folded tightly against their chest in the defensive mode, both nursing a look of hurt petulance. While Noel was eager to enter into conversation, any conversation, he believed that, as the subordinate, it was up to Simon to make the first move which, to Noel's profound relief, Simon eventually made.

After a sigh of resignation Simon unfolded is arms, closed his eyes tightly and ran a hand across his face. 'I s'pose you're wondering what that was all about?' he said bleakly. 'No, don't answer that 'cause I'm wondering myself.'

'Well, I was, sorta. Here we are in the middle of some gruesome murders and I get the idea you've either gone off your rocker or you're not really interested.'

Simon shrugged. 'Yeah, you're probably right on that score, but before this discussion gets any deeper, maybe we should get a few things clear. What goes on in this office stays in this office. However, the main point I wish to make, and if you're not happy with it just say so, is that we drop the yes, sir, yes sir, three bags full bit and have a little heart to heart as the friends we are.'

'Fine, I'll go along with that. In fact, I'm happy to do so. Right from the start of this investigation something seems to have gone wrong and maybe a good old heart to heart might be something we both need,' Noel replied, somewhat gratified that at least the ice had been broken.

Simon sat back and slowly shook his head and contemplated where to start. 'Noel, I might be the senior officer in the room at the moment, but I have a burning question to which I have no answer. That question is, what the hell are we doing here as it all seems such a waste of time? Sure, there's crime running rampant in the streets but the majority of that is at the lower level of the scale, such as the Benny and Jacko debacle down at that pub at The Rocks. Yeah, there's a stack of murders being committed but most of those seem to be domestic or drug related. The murders we're saddled with at the moment have opened a Pandora's box of high flying politicians, unscrupulous developers and, to top that off, members of a Chinese triad organisation out to buy up as much of the city as they can get their hands on.'

Noel nodded in agreement. 'Yep, I totally agree, but we

still have a job to do and along with the job comes the satisfaction of getting a conviction, sometimes.'

'And there you have hit the nail on the head. We work our butts off to get a case to court and that's where everything falls to pieces. The legal process is nothing more than a sham between two teams; the good guys try to get the bad guys behind bars while the bad guys do everything they can to avoid being put there. It's up to us, as the good guys, to scrape all the evidence we can muster to convince a jury that the bad guys are as bad as we make them out to be. On the other hand, the bad guys, depending on their financial situation, can go and hire a barrister who charges a zillion dollars a day but has never lost a case. Now, getting back to our particular investigation, all our suspects have the assets to hire some super-duper legal eagle which means that no matter how guilty the rotters are, they'll get off scot-free.'

'So again, I agree with you,' came Noel's concise response. 'The problem for the good guys is that the deck is stacked against them and getting worse. Soon it will be impossible to get a conviction against a homicidal maniac such as Norman Bates.'

'Norman Bates?'

'Yeah, the psycho bloke who owned the motel,' Noel replied. 'But as I said, with all the do-gooders beating their drum, the good guys are pushing the proverbial up hill. Even now, you only have to look at the sentences being handed down to wonder if it's all worthwhile. And just what do you have in mind 'cause if it's what I think it is, I'm with you? I reckon we did a real neat trick on that bank job, and it was rather exciting.'

'Yeah, but this wouldn't be a one-off thing; it would be a career move,' Simon explained. 'No violence or murder stuff or anything like that. It's all a bit of a pipe-dream at the moment but it's something I want to have a good think about. What d'you say?'

'Does it mean leaving the force?'

'Not immediately. I'd have to see how it pans out. But that's one of the things I have to think about.'

'No,' came Noel's abrupt and adamant response, 'we have to think about'.

Chapter 33

Simon and Noel relaxed on the lounge chairs and looked on as Graham Lee attended to the provision of some light refreshments; two Foster's lagers and a Johnny Walker. Although it was still in the ante meridiem, but having anticipated Graham would be in his office at the Taipan Club because of circumstances, the two detectives, dressed in mufti, had made their unannounced call to ascertain if there had been any developments involving the future of the club. In addition, and since Graham was always walking the fine line between legal and illegal pursuits, he was well placed to hear of any underworld prattle relating to the three murders currently under investigation.

'Something must be rotten somewhere to bring you out at this early hour,' Graham chided, fully aware of Simon's propensity to sprout the Bard, incorrectly.'

'And how's that?' Simon inquired as he took the offered glass of beer.

'It's just that I don't think I've ever seen you have a beer while on duty, and it is before lunchtime.'

'Yeah, well things seem to be getting a bit out of hand and we need some fortification,' Simon replied.

Having placed his whisky on the coffee table, Graham relaxed in a somewhat leisurely manner on the three-seater lounge, kicked off his slip-on shoes, removed his tie and undid the top button of his shirt. Yep, casual be to he who casual thinks, thought Simon.

'Okay, Simon, and just what is it that's getting out of hand?' Graham asked.

Simon set his glass down, heaved a sigh and sat back, hands clasped, his arched thumbs tapping together. 'We think we have the Morton Blakey murder under control, not that we're inundated with hard evidence, 'though I s'pose a speeding train is probably as hard a piece of evidence you'll find,' Simon added as an afterthought. 'The death of his wife, Rosetta, is a bit more complicated and a case of "he said, she said", with a bit of circumstantial evidence thrown in. We think David Zheng's death can be attributed to John Chang although, again, we don't have any evidence to prove it one way or the other. But that's beside the point as we didn't come here to talk about our problems, we came to see you about your problems. So, just what is the state of play at the moment?'

Graham nodded as he gathered his thoughts together. 'Well, things seem pretty weird right now. Despite the fact that Gem Property Development is undergoing some turmoil at the management level, it looks like the government is hell bent on getting their overseas ownership bill through parliament as soon as possible. Once they get that sorted out, Gem will be in here so fast I won't have time to clear out my desk. Unfortunately, without Blakey around to cross the floor, that scenario seems to be a foregone conclusion. Gem thinks it's a fait accompli and are working on that assumption. I think I've already resigned myself to the fact I'll be dropping at least a million bucks as government compensation for the acquisition of the property will be a pittance compared to the market value. And you don't have to be Einstein to work out that the government will sell it on to this overseas mob for about five times the amount I'll receive, which will still be at a bargain price. But the real loss is not being able to fulfil the deal with Henry. I know he can be a cantankerous sod at times, but I like the bloke and feel sorry for the predicament I've put him in. And all because we have a politician who's getting buckets of money from some overseas criminal group to do what they want him to do, which could amount to anything.'

'You mean he's getting a kick-back?' Noel ventured to ask.

'Of course he is, but no names, no pack drill, so don't quote me,' Graham returned with a wry grin. 'Anyway, I'm sure you're fully aware of who the "he" is.'

Simon finished off the remainder of his beer and placed the glass on the coffee table. 'So, what does the future hold for Graham Lee now?' he asked.

Graham gave a "wouldn't have a clue" shrug along with the appropriate animated expression. 'Although the club may appear to be my sole source of revenue, I do have other irons in the fire that will keep me out of the workhouse. I enjoy running the place here and I'll feel the loss, but more out of sentimentality than anything else. One of the things that sticks in my craw is the length some people will go to make a few extra bucks, and that includes setting new laws in place to facilitate their nefarious activities, exactly as they're doing now.'

'So, have you considered a change?' Simon casually posed.

'A change?' Graham asked, his interest piqued by the odd question.

'From good to bad, not that bad should be construed as being really bad, just Robin Hood type bad,' Simon clarified, 'and against specifically targeted individuals, of course.'

Graham nodded his understanding of the situation. Simon, and presumably Noel as well, must be pretty fed up with trying to catch murderers for whom they couldn't care less whether they caught them or not. And I can see where they're coming from, Graham thought. The law says things are either legal or illegal, but nobody pays any attention to those virtuous attributes people used to possess in the good old days of the distant past. 'Interesting thought, Simon. Someone said revenge is best served cold but maybe served whenever the opportunity presents itself would suffice, and there's a few people who need serving. But what about your current problem?'

Simon heaved a sigh. 'Yeah, as Fisher's on our backs to get some results, the longer we can stay out of his hair, the better. As you said, there seems to be something going on with Jezebel and Daniel Dawkins over at Gem. Daniel says he's being poisoned by Jezebel, and he certainly looks like someone is poisoning him, or she's a very bad cook. Jezebel says it's a load of garbage; what Daniel claims, not her cooking. Anyway, if he does drop dead, good old Jezebel would become head of Gem, if she's not convicted of murder.'

'But even if she was, she'd be out of jail in no time flat, pockets Daniel's bank account and takes over the business. Sorta like having your cake and eating it too,' Noel added sarcastically.

'And wouldn't our Mr Chang love that,' Graham interjected.

Simon looked at Noel who returned his gaze with a reciprocal look of awakened intuitive thinking of a thought not previously contemplated; John Chang and Jezebel Dawkins. 'We're aware Mr Chang and Jezebel have a thing going but a joint business venture would really be something else,' Noel asserted. 'But, heavens to Murgatroyd, Graham, how did you come up with that little gem of corporate insight?

'Simple,' Graham replied nonchalantly, 'human nature. Jezebel and Daniel aren't getting on too well together and along comes Grasshopper with all the charm and charisma of Errol Flynn. Personally, I think Chang has neither a caring bone in his body nor anything you could call a conscience;

nice as pie one minute and Jack the Ripper the next. However, I think Jezebel knows exactly what side her bread is buttered and is in the process of doing a bit more buttering.'

'And where do you suppose that will leave Daniel?' Simon asked.

Graham struggled from the settee and picked up the three empty glasses. 'I'll think about that while I get some more fortification,' he said as he padded his shoeless way to the small bar fridge. On his return, he deposited the glasses on the coffee table and readopted his previous casual seating position. 'Everything is highly speculative as far as I can determine in regards to your murders, and now you tell me Daniel believes he's in the process of getting himself poisoned. He must be pretty whacko if he believes Jezebel is feeding him rat poison and chooses not to do anything about it, while Jezebel must be whacko if she doesn't believe she'll get done for murder if she is, feeding him poison, I mean. According to you, Jezebel has already stated that she won't be giving up Daniel unless it's to her financial advantage, and Chang might be the person with the money to make that happen.'

Noel rested his elbow on the chair arm-rest and held his head in his hand. 'Yeah well, it all seems too obvious to be real for me. If Jezebel gets rid of Daniel that would open the door for Jezebel, as boss of Gem, to team up with Chang. With his endless supply of money and the burning desire of his colleagues back in Honkers to buy every piece of real estate they can get their hands on, Jezebel would be laughing all the way to the bank. And once the Premier gets his bill passed, which will set a precedence for further overseas acquisitions, you can bet he's not going to disclose his Chang sourced burgeoning pecuniary interests under the parliamentary Code of Conduct conditions, as he's required to do. No, that'll be one source of income the Premier will choose to keep very hush hush.'

'Yeah okay, but our prognostication on what might happen

is predicated on the assumption Daniel will be dead,' Simon mumbled. 'And we don't really know if he is actually being poisoned as Jezebel really might be a bad cook. He wasn't in the best of health when we took him over to the hospital where he was admitted. The doctors said they'd run some tests and pump him out if the need arises but, so far, we haven't received any news back on his condition. Anyway, there's no reason why Gem shouldn't be counting on Chang's ongoing support irrespective of who's head of the company, Daniel or Jezebel. He needs a developer just as much as a developer needs the cashed-up entrepreneur. I'm sure Chang couldn't care less if he's dealing with Jezebel or Daniel, although I bet Jezebel would prefer to be Chang's preferred confidante.'

'I'm sorry, Simon, but I detect a degree of ambivalence and have this odd idea you haven't put your heart and soul into this investigation. Am I being a bit judgmental or have you lost your mojo?' Graham queried in a hesitant manner, not wishing to offer offence.

Simon heaved a sigh and shook his head. 'Is it any wonder? We go to all this trouble to find the homicidal maniacs knowing full well that, even if we get them to court, nothing's going to happen even if they're found guilty. Anyway, Graham, what do you reckon?'

'About what?'

'Changing sides,'

Graham looked contemplative for a moment before downing the remains of his whisky. 'Simon, I'm not going to reject the offer out of hand, but I'd like to think about it and wait to see what happens here. Leave it with us and I'll get back to you on that one.'

Chapter 34

Including the uninvited interloper, currently waddling along the top of the fence for a more favourable position to view the expected arrival of beak-watering nibblies, the number congregated on Simon's back lawn had grown from the initial thirteen to fourteen, not that anyone had taken the time to notice Johnathon L, the silver seagull; well, not yet, anyway. As the gull was such a frequent visitor to the back yard of 24 West Bank Lane, Simon believed it appropriate to give the interloper a name with Georgie coming up with the appropriate, and very fitting, title.

None of the eleven guests felt put out by Simon and Georgie's invitation, albeit for a Sunday afternoon, usually the leisure time set aside to follow one's inclination wherever it might lead. However, the majority of the invitees probably anticipated, or at least harboured a smidgen of optimism, that the recent eventful episodes of murder and mayhem would be the prime topic of discussion with the possibility of explanations, revelations and a lot of finger-pointing, contributing to the afternoon's entertainment. As a consequence, anyone with previous arrangements for this particular Sunday quickly shelved their plans in preference to an afternoon of sipping a quiet chardonnay, or the light amber, and listening to a gripping piece of tittle-tattle.

There were those guests who had previously visited 24 West Bank Lane by invitation, namely Noel, Ron and Graham Lee with their respective spouses, or likely spouse in Ron's case. In addition, there were two visitors with an intimate knowledge of West Bank Lane, Jacko and Benny who, following a visit to 24 West Bank Lane, had agreed to take whatever steps necessary to ensure that the tenanted occupants of 26 West Bank Lane were suitably informed and under no illusion that it might be in their best interest to relocate from Collaroy.

The request for such harsh but necessary action was made in the belief, primarily Georgie's, that the occupants were cultivating marijuana and were members of some radical bikie gang. Needless to say, things didn't quite go to plan and it was 24 West Bank Lane that was subjected to a cataclysmic night time ride-by twelve-gauge shotgun blast. Well, as far as Simon and Georgie were concerned, the demolition of their bungalow's front window was a cataclysmic event. However, a subsequent ride-by molotov cocktail attack, albeit somewhat excessive, achieved the desired effect with the residents choosing to leave 26 West Bank Lane, the dwelling having been burnt to the ground.

The remaining three visitors who had never been to West Bank Lane, and probably had never ventured further north than the harbour bridge, were Inspector Dave Harris from the Kings Cross Local Area Command, Jackie from the Premier's office up in Macquarie Street and Henry Haynes from Glover Property Development located in Bondi Junction. While the others probably had an inkling of what might be the subject of discussion, Jackie and Henry remained totally in the dark, albeit more than happy to enjoy the congenial company and imbibe in the occasional Barossa sauvignon blanc beverage, a rare occurrence for the cantankerous Henry.

Simon, in anticipation of a prolonged discussion concerning two separate, but not totally unrelated topics, decided it was time to open proceedings. 'Ladies and gentleman,' he announced in a raised and authoritative voice aimed to draw attention away from the small-talk and chit-chat going on. Once silence had been achieved, Simon continued. 'First off, thanks for coming over and a special welcome to Henry, Dave, and especially Jackie who probably hasn't a clue as to what this is all about.'

'Gee, sir, you got that one right, but if this is how you spend your Sunday afternoons, I expect a few more invites,' Jackie entreated with a broad smile.

'Hey, just cut that out, Jackie. There's no rank or "sirs" here, so it's Simon,' Simon admonished. 'But let's get on with the first thing on the agenda and the subject you all want to talk about; the spate of murders recently perpetrated. From the outset, I should warn you that we would be pushing the proverbial up hill to proceed to a trial in any of these cases as much of the evidence is circumstantial and the motive nothing more than speculation. I very much doubt any of the cases would get past the preliminary hearing stage. Even if we did get across that bridge, it would come down to being a complete waste of time and effort as we hold very little confidence in the judiciaries ability to pass a sentence commensurate with the crime committed. But let's get on with what we think we know and if anyone can see a gaping hole in our estimation of events, please feel free to intervene. We'll start with the first casualty off the rank, Morton Blakey who, as you are all aware, was knifed in the back and thrown in front of a train.'

It was Ron who, having just pulled a can of beer from the esky, interjected. 'Yeah, but we all know Rosetta and David Zheng were the villains in this case.'

'Maybe, maybe not,' Simon responded. 'I'll go along with Zheng's involvement as he ended up being somewhere between the hammer and the anvil.'

Graham Lee looked at Simon with a quizzical look. 'Okay, we know Zheng had motive for doing away with Blakey, but most people would let the situation ride and be happy to see what happens whenever Fortesque's bill is reintroduced to parliament. How does that leave Zheng on the anvil?'

'Yes, most people would be happy to maintain the status quo, but poor Mr Zheng had his boss, John Chang, to contend with. Zheng felt he had to at least display some sort of initiative as a result of Blakey's action so, as there was no-one else around to get up Zheng's nose, Morton Blakey had to go. What we don't know is whether Zheng had revenge in mind or just wanted to eliminate the hiccup currently delaying the government takeover of the Taipan Club and its subsequent sale to the Hong Kong enterprise. But that's beside the point. I think it safe to say Zheng was involved in Blakey's death, irrespective of his motive.

'The question is, who was he involved with. We all seem to think it was Rosetta who really found out what she had married. And yes, Rosetta was peeved to think she wasn't worth a plugged nickel to dear sweet hubby.'

'Yeah, Mrs Blakey certainly had her nose put out of joint. Maybe it was a good thing we did stuff up that kidnapping or she would never have found out what she wasn't worth,' Benny managed to blurt out before letting loose an infectious guffaw.

'Yeah, well thanks, Benny,' Simon said, acknowledging both Benny's and Jacko's role in kickstarting a bout of serial killings. 'While Rosetta may have had motive for killing off her husband, it is my contention that Zheng's accomplice was none other than Jezebel Dawkins.'

Letting his statement sink in, Simon surveyed the circle of

confused faces while Johnathon L, totally unfazed as to what was going on around him, continued his waddle under the chairs and table seeking the odd tit-bit of goodies that may come his way. Although unrehearsed, Sue, Judy and Louisa all posed the same question at precisely the same time, - 'Jezebel Dawkins??'

Simon rose from his director's chair, clasped his hands behind his back and, with head down and eyes fixed to the ground, started to stroll slowly around the seated circle of inquisitive guests. 'Yes, my friends, Jezebel Dawkins. During the last election Jezebel, as Morton's campaign manager, had been eager to provide Morton Blakey with additional benefits of a personal nature, quite apart from a campaign strategy. Unfortunately, for Jezebel, this arrangement apparently turned out more one sided than she hoped it would be.

'It was only after a successful campaign and Morton's election to parliament that Morton, having no further use for Jezebel, gave her the old heave-ho, a bit of the old "keep 'em keen, then treat 'em mean" performance. This meant Jezebel had to be satisfied with her substantially wealthy hubby, Daniel, who, by the by, was having it off in a torrid affair with Rosetta. But any jilted woman, once unceremoniously cast aside, believes she is handed justifiable grounds to seek horrible and permanent retribution on the deceitful, scurrilous degenerate. Vindication for such extreme action is usually enhanced when the "he" in the relationship has declared his undying love and expressed his sincere intention to flog off the current wife, in this case Rosetta, and marry the gullible mistress, in this case, Jezebel, which is all par for the course for the married man seeking nothing more than a bit on the side. With an ounce of luck, any self-respecting presiding judge might consider Jezebel's retribution an act of justifiable homicide and award the femme fatale a merit badge, irrespective of just how provocative and enticing the fair Jezebel might have appeared to the rapacious Romeo. If you're looking for a motive for murder, just remember, nor hell a fury like a woman scorned, or words to that effect.'

Louisa, who had been a close friend of both Rosetta and Jezebel, scrutinised the remaining chardonnay in her glass with a concentrated gaze. Finally, having arrived at the patently obvious conclusion, she addressed Simon as he continued his stroll. 'Okay Simon, Jezebel meets Zheng over at Gem where they eventually start talking about, among other things, their respective reasons for displeasure towards Morton Blakey. It is during one such conversation that the seed, having already been planted, culminates in both Jezebel and Zheng sticking a knife into Morton and pushing him out in from of the 3.30 to Milson's Point.'

Simon stopped his strolling and, with his back to Louisa and hands still firmly clasped behind him, listened to her abridged version of Morton's death. On completion of Louisa's appraisal of events, he immediately did a parade ground about turn. 'Louisa, according to my estimation, you've hit the nail on the head which is probably a little less dramatic than what hit Morton. Okay, can anyone see any major blunders?'

Simon was not overwhelmed by the immediate response from anyone in his audience, all of whom had gone to great pains to listen to Simon's extended account of the death of Morton Blakey, MP. It was left to Dave Harris who, with years of policing and murder investigations under his belt, felt obliged to alleviate an embarrassing prolonged silence and add his experience to Simon's evaluation of events. 'While not having had any involvement in the investigation, it sounds good to me, Simon,' he said with a shrug and a bemused look.

'Well, thanks for agreeing with me, Dave. In view of the silence, I take it the rest of you have no comment to make and agree with my speculation, which is what it is; mere speculation,' Simon said before making his way to the esky for a refreshingly cold can of beer. After quenching his thirst after his long-winded address, he regained his director's chair and looked to Noel, nodded and gave an invitational wave of the hand.

Chapter 35

Noel tossed his empty beer can into the garbage bin and stood to address the expectant gathering. 'Now that Simon has covered the first murder to have been successfully carried out, let us turn our attention to murder number two, which may have been murder number three, but let's not quibble about who got done first, Rosetta or David Zheng but, for argument's sake, we'll assume Mr Zheng got done first.

'Both Mr Zheng and Mr Chang who, as it turns out, members of a triad organisation based in Hong Kong, came to Sydney with the expressed purpose of establishing, or controlling, a property development company here in Sydney. While we initially thought Zheng was Mr Brains of the operation, it was really Cheng holding the reins while overseeing Zheng's performance in real estate negotiations with a possible promotion for Zheng in the triad organisation. I will neither go into the ramifications of the ownership of property sold off to overseas buyers, nor the consequences of overseas ownership of a city based property development company ready to redevelop any of the overseas owned properties.

'The first step in this fiasco, as you're all aware, relate to the acquisition of Graham's Taipan Club site by an overseas cartel, and the subsequent construction of a six-star hotel complex. The actual construction of the hotel has already been placed in the hands of Gem Development under the management of Daniel and Jezebel Dawkins who have taken out an injunction against Graham preventing him from proceeding with his plans for a residential complex. Unfortunately, Henry here,' Noel paused and nodded to Henry Haynes, 'in collaboration with Graham, had already submitted preliminary plans to council for the construction of a residential complex in anticipation of the club being sold to Henry.

'Irrespective of whatever plans for the redevelopment of the site are in the pipeline, be they Graham's or this overseas mob, progress has come to an abrupt halt, thanks to Morton Blakey and his opposition to the Premier sponsored Foreign Ownership Bill. Now, although Mr Zheng was doing all the footwork for the Hong Kong based conglomerate, it was, as I said, Mr Chang who was really the boss. While Jezebel and Zheng were plotting to do away with Blakey during Zheng's visits to Gem Development, with Chang tagging along to assess Zheng's negotiating skills, Chang was making goo-goo eyes at Jezebel with the possibility of a future liaison in mind, notwithstanding Chang had an ulterior motive for chatting up Jezebel.

'Anyway, Zheng's death. Zheng had been happy to help Jezebel get rid of Blakey as he believed it would prove to Chang that he had the intestinal fortitude to make it in the world of the triad. Needless to say, Mr Chang didn't quite see it that way and blamed Zheng for the delay in procuring the Taipan Club. As a consequence, Zheng had to go. As Chang was busy elsewhere at the time of Zheng's death, we believe Chang conscripted a local triad member to do the job which was carried out in a customary triad method. Needless to say, no-one can provide any information as to exactly who wielded the blade and we doubt if further investigation would prove fruitful.

'Following the death of Zheng, Chang took over negotiations with the Premier and Gem. During his not infrequent visits to the Premier's office, as Jackie here can verify,' Noel again paused to nod to Jackie who was enjoying another chardonnay, 'the Premier provided Chang assurances that everything was hunky-dory but he would still need continued remuneration for his efforts to find a suitable candidate to fulfil Blakey's vacant seat in parliament. That in itself would be no easy task as Blakey's replacement had to be a compliant member of the party, if for no other reason than to ensure the Foreign Ownership Bill would be passed.'

'Yes, but what about Rosetta?' Louisa asked. 'We now know who killed Morton and who was responsible for Mr Zheng's death, which I suppose is tolerably interesting. However, as I regarded Rosetta as a friend, I can't help feeling responsible for her death in some way having suggested what she might do with Morton, and killing him wasn't a suggestion.'

'Okay, let's talk about Rosetta,' Noel, standing at ease with his feet firmly planted apart in a display of confidence, hands clasped firmly together in front of himself, as taught by his instructional staff at the academy, announced with his gaze fixed on Louisa. 'Rosetta was dunked into the harbour by none other than Mr Chang and Jezebel Dawkins.'

Louisa, somewhat perplexed, shook her head in a show of scepticism. 'But why? I thought Rosetta and Jezebel got on well together despite the fact that both were sleeping with the other's husband, a situation both women were fully aware of.'

Noel relaxed his stance and, with a demonstrative wave of the hand to emphasise the point, said, 'Yes, that may have been the case. However, before we proceed, we should understand a few things. Despite Jezebel's assertion that Rosetta couldn't lie straight in bed, it was Jezebel herself who was far more adroit at spinning the odd porky than Rosetta. So, whatever Jezebel has said in the past should be taken with a degree of scepticism as her veracity is questionable. In order that Rosetta's death may be understood more clearly, it is necessary to spend some time on the relationship between Mr Chang and Mrs Dawkins.'

Interest in the circle of visitors had waned after Simons lengthy disclosure on the death of Morton Blakey. However, after a brief but fascinating account of David Zheng's death, Noel's introduction into the death of Morton Blakey's wife provoked a keen interest in an audience anxious for the whys and the wherefores relating to the death of the woman known to many sitting in a circle on Simon's back lawn, Rosetta Blakey.

'As Louisa has already pointed out,' Noel continued, 'Rosetta and Jezebel had an agreement whereupon they could bed the others husband. I must point out that we don't know if either of the husbands were acquainted with the rules of their wife's little agreement. Anyway, it seems one side of this arrangement ended when Morton gave Jezebel the flick at a time while Daniel and Rosetta were continuing their little tryst. In fact, I think they would probably have still been at it as Rosetta harboured thoughts of a permanent arrangement with Daniel. It just so happens that any ideas Rosetta may have been contemplating regarding the snaring Daniel as hubby number three came to an abrupt halt when she drowned.

'Irrespective of whether Morton and Daniel were aware of their participation in an agreed mixed foursome or not, it seems the relationship between Rosetta and Daniel Dawkins was getting a bit beyond the women's agreed rules, at least as perceived by Jezebel. In fact, many of the phone calls made by Rosetta during her kidnapping were to Daniel. As Jezebel had already stated that she would never give up Daniel unless it was worth her while to do so, the relationship between Daniel and Rosetta was seen by Jezebel as a threat to her attaining Daniel's not insignificant wealth should they decide sometime down the road to tie the knot. Keeping that in mind, Jezebel was, understandably, becoming a little agitated.

And it's here that John Chang started to surreptitiously assert his influence. If successful in his endeavours to establish a Chinese managed property development company in the heart of Sydney town, his triad bosses back in Honk Kong would probably give him a merit award and catapult him up the prestigious organisational ladder. To help achieve his aim, Chang needed the support of two people; political support, which was obtained from a politician already in the process of being handsomely remunerated, and the support of someone in the property development industry, Jezebel Dawkins from Gem Development.

'Chang believed Jezebel could be easily enticed to provide the support needed after a bit of romantic wooing, especially in light of her current matrimonial situation, not that he ever mentioned anything to her about his own intentions. From our personal observation I think it safe to say Chang was perfectly correct in his appraisal of Jezebel's susceptibility to a bit of wooing.

'Chang had discretely planted the notion in Jezebel's mind that Gem would be better off without Daniel and that she should do something about it. Once that idea had been firmly imbedded, and the fact that Daniel's fortune stood to be usurped by Rosetta, a predicament that didn't sit well with Jezebel, Jezebel took umbrage to the whole affair and decided some remedial action was required.

'Don't forget, Daniel always claimed Jezebel was poisoning him whereas we all thought it was just a case of bad cooking. Anyway, it seems that Jezebel was, in fact, feeding hubby small doses of poison in his food. Daniel eventually yielded to Jezebel's culinary delights but, fortunately for him, we were able to get him off to a hospital before reaching the point of no return. While we initially may have thought Daniel's claims a bit over the top, he was correct as doctors at the hospital later confirmed he was suffering from arsenic trioxide poisoning.

'The whole idea behind this masterful piece of homicidal lunacy was Jezebel's plan to take over Gem Development and pocket Daniel's own substantial wealth. Needless to say, Chang was fully aware of Jezebel's poisoning of Daniel as it was Chang himself who suggested to Jezebel that Daniel's wealth would look better in her bank account than Daniel's. However, in view of his own undisclosed intentions relating to the future of Gem, he was more than happy not to rock the boat and said nothing that may have jeopardised Jezebel's ambition. Despite her designs on the company, and quite unbeknownst to Jezebel, Mr Chang had his own ideas as to who should run Gem Development. Now that we have covered the essential background details according to our expert guesswork, we will take a short break before dealing with the murder of Rosetta Blakey.'

The attentive audience, that had remained attentive despite the length of Noel's spiel of the perceived sordid goings on, welcomed the opportunity to take a trip to the loo, grab a handful of nibblies, or organise another glass of wine or whatever held their fancy. Louisa, in deep conversation with Graham, still looked perplexed even though she now appreciated the fact that Jezebel probably had her own good reasons for the killing off of Rosetta and her attempt to do away with Daniel.

'Noel, before you get started,' Louisa, having turned to face the detective, implored, 'I concede Jezebel probably, in her own mind, had good reason to kill Rosetta. But this gets back to motive, which is one of the three aspects of proving a crime. How do you prove the motive angle as it seems to me very subjective and one that can only be truthfully answered by the criminal himself or, in this case, herself?'

Noel turned to Simon who, intrigued by both the question and eager to hear what Noel's educated answer might be, leaned forward on his chair, elbows on his knees while his hands clutched a can of larger. 'Oh, come on boss, maybe Louisa's right and all this stuff about motive, means and opportunity is a load of garbage,' Noel said dubiously. 'After all, everyone on that railway platform probably had the means and opportunity to kill off Morton as everyone would have access to a knife of some sort and the opportunity was there to throw him out onto the trainline. However, we immediately discount the multitude as we can't see that anyone would have a motive.'

Simon nodded his understanding of Noel's predicament before responding to his subordinate's request for help. 'And I totally agree with Louisa,' Simon said. 'It seems the good guys, namely us, only have to come up with a plausible motive for a particular crime whereas, in reality, that plausible motive may never have entered the head of the suspect in the first place and might be seen by the suspect as a total fabrication. All the police can do is find a reason, any reason, why the suspect of a crime would want to carry out a particular felony. Once a reasonable motive has been dreamt up, the motive aspect of the crime has been satisfied while, in reality, the particular motive determined by the police may never have entered the mind of the suspect in the first place.'

'I think I'll take a headache pill,' Noel responded, not quite sure if Simon had been any help. Turning to Louisa, Noel said apologetically, 'I'm sorry for the absence of a simple answer to your question, Louisa, but maybe Simon was able to explain the unexplainable a hell of a lot better than I would have been able.'

'No, that's fine, Noel. I just couldn't see how we can say someone has a motive unless we're inside their head,' Louisa replied.

Despite Louisa's purely unintentional attack on Noel's

credibility, Noel started to pace around the circle of happily imbibing visitors to West Bank Lane, his hands clasped firmly behind his back in an outward display of a growing confidence following his exhibition of motive motivated ignorance. 'Right, now as you're all waiting in fervent anticipation for the details of Rosetta's death, we shall proceed.

'Chang clearly recognised the fact that his involvement in Gem Development, once Jezebel had provided Daniel with the final dose of arsenic, would be dependent on his successful cultivation of his relationship with Jezebel. Chang, loaded up with charm, charisma and cash, set out to win fair maiden, a move Daniel expected Jezebel would be quite amenable to, and was.

'While we know Chang was aware of Jezebel's plot to do Daniel irreparable damage, he also knew Jezebel was out to make sure Rosetta didn't get her claws into Daniel's wealth. The one thing he probably didn't know, initially at least, was just how far Jezebel would go to make sure Rosetta didn't. With Daniel's sizeable bank account at stake, Jezebel was faced with some sort of a dilemma; get rid of Rosetta or get rid of Daniel before he had time to change both his wife and his will. Confronted with this unforeseen conundrum and unable to make up her mind, Jezebel took the only action she believed would solve the problem; she decided to do both of them in. Chang, on the other hand, wasn't duly worried about Daniel's personal wealth, as Jezebel was; he had his sights set on becoming the head honcho of Gem Development.

'Now', Noel continued, 'to eliminate any possible inconvenience Rosetta might create while Jezebel took control of Gem Development, both Jezebel and Chang finally conspired to do away with Rosetta, although for very different reasons. As Chang wanted to remove any possible obstruction to his plot to eventually take control of Gem himself, he was quite happy to lend his support to Jezebel for the removal of Rosetta. In fact, he believed that by helping Jezebel kill

Rosetta he would further ingratiate himself with Jezebel and improve his chances of a position within Gem once Daniel was dead and Jezebel had become head of the company.

'Jezebel had already started the poisoning process of Daniel although the extent of Daniel's burgeoning relationship with Rosetta presented Chang with the concern that Rosetta may later prove to be a fly in his ointment. Under the circumstances, Chang was quite happy to help Jezebel eliminate Rosetta. With Jezebel already having murdered Blakey, and Chang being a triad gang member and having organised the death of Zheng, another murder or two appeared to be of little consequence to either cold-blooded, calculating assassin. In any case, Chang had already decided Jezebel could be taken care of later, if need be.

'On the night of the murder, Jezebel and Chang drove independently over to Rushcutter Bay where they met before boarding Graham Lee's boat, *Gemini*. I will not go into the sordid details of the actual murder, save to say that Rosetta was known for her inability to swim. Following a glass of wine or two, and what appeared to be a quiet social get-together, Rosetta was heaved overboard from *Gemini* and, with a bit of encouragement to stay in the water, helped by a bit of prodding with a boathook, she finally drowned.'

Jacko, who had been listening intently to Noel's revelation of the suspected sequence of events, could see a profound question needed to be addressed. Despite Jacko's reputation as not being the brightest light on the Christmas tree, he was not alone in questioning the obvious. 'Okay Noel, before you go any further, there seems to be a lot of questions that could be answered either by Chang or Jezebel. But the first question should be, why haven't they been arrested as they have both been directly involved in two of the three murders? Surely the police had sufficient evidence to have both Chang and Jezebel hung, drawn and quartered.'

'And that, Jacko,' Noel, now standing with arms akimbo,

announced, 'is the very reason why you have all been invited here today. Each of you bring to this circle either the knowledge and experience that we think may be needed to assist us, or are in a position to obtain certain information that may be of value and worth pursuing. As we have cleared up the "who did what to whom", Simon wishes to say a few words and present a proposal to you all. I think you will find it both interesting and different, to say the least.'

'Hang on a moment,' Henry interjected. 'What about Graham's club and all the trouble I've gone through with the submission of plans to council?'

Noel turned to Henry and, with an animated nod to emphasise the point he wished to make. 'A very valid question, Henry, which leads us to the crux of the matter that Simon will address.'

Chapter 36

Simon didn't rise from his chair, preferring to remain seated to address the expectant multitude that continued to include Johnathon L who had made up his mind that he wasn't going anywhere while there were still a few crumbs of sustenance to be pecked. 'As you are all probably aware, right from the beginning of this investigation I haven't been over endowed with enthusiasm. This lack of commitment to the case, or cases, was probably brought on by a lack of respect for those involved in the property development industry, no offence meant, Henry, and for my perception of the politicians' seemingly lack of integrity and altruistic motivation. On top of that, we have what I believe is a judiciary out of touch with reality. It seems hardly worth while spending so much time and effort getting a case to trial only to find that the perpetrator of some trivial offence, such as the premeditated murder of some poor innocent sod, is out on the streets having been sentenced to a two year good behaviour bond.'

Dave Harris, who had sat in silence enjoying the occasional beer and friendly atmosphere, nodded in acknowledgement of Simon's castigation of the judiciary. 'Yeah well, don't think you're on your Pat Malone on that score, Simon. Fortunately I'm due for retirement soon which means I won't have to put up with all the stupidity that goes on. But I agree with you, along with the majority of people. A slap on the wrist, which appears to be the only sentence imposed from J-walking to murder, is no inducement for a criminal to change his ways. It's certainly not like in the old US of A where if you do the crime, you do the time. I, for one, applaud their sentencing procedure which appears to be determined by the seriousness of the crime committed; life means life and once the guilty is incarcerated they throw away the keys.'

'Yeah, well that's all well and good, but I'm not fussed about pursuing Chang and Jezebel,' Simon said dismissively. 'I have no doubt Chang who, if not guilty of murder is at least guilty of being an accessory, has already made an approach to the Premier, and any action taken against Chang would probably provoke some sort of international crisis. Needless to say, Jezebel's unsuccessful attempt to poison Daniel resulted in Daniel giving her the sack in absentia as both Chang and Jezebel have disappeared off the face of the earth. I have absolutely no idea where Jezebel or her boyfriend is and, to tell the truth, I don't really give a damn.'

Having discreetly removed himself from the group to answer his mobile phone, Ron now returned and maintained his chair. 'My apologies, Simon, but I just received a bit of information regarding Chang. There's a rumour going around China Town that Chang has blotted his copy-book big time. Apparently the Taipan Club takeover has been seen by those in Hong Kong to have turned into a complete fiasco and, while Chang got rid of Zheng and Zheng got rid of Blakey, there's now a contract out on Chang. I somehow think planet Earth holds no hiding place for Chang no matter where or how far he runs. Whether he's accompanied by Jezebel is a moot point. And don't get yourself into a tizz 'cause this info is hot off the press,' Ron elaborated, just in case.

Simon rocked back on his chair, arms folded; he was gobsmacked. 'And thank you, Ron, for that most illuminating piece of information. It's really refreshing to know that we have two potential murderers running around. I say "potential" only because it's politically correct not to condemn them before a trial, although we know they're both as guilty as hell.

'But this is where it gets up my nose,' Simon continued in frustration. 'People who commit criminal acts, such as Chang and Jezebel, get charged under the Crimes Act which covers a multitude of sins and we, the police, are out to catch those who commit offences in breach of the Act. Now, to my mind that's clear enough; if someone bashes someone over the head with a baseball bat, the basher is in breach of the Crimes Act and should be dealt with accordingly.

'However, there is no accountability for those people in public office who believe it their sole given right to perform their duties while totally devoid of any scruples, ethics, moral standards and any other personal attribute by which the character of a person was once assessed. And how often do we hear the bureaucrat say "I've done nothing wrong", referring to the legality of his actions while he totally dismisses the ethical issues. We see it every day; a politician scrounging the system for all it's worth and lining his pockets with jaunts on the gravy train, or a property developer paying the politician oodles of cash for a favour.

'This latest case we've been investigating is a classic example with Chang paying off the Premier for a decision that would be financially beneficial to Gem Development, Chang and the politician. And getting back to your question, Henry, as far as we know, everything has stalled until the Premier finds someone to fill the vacancy brought about by Blakey's death. Once he's done that, he'll get his bill passed and I'd say you'll be out of a job and Graham out of the Taipan Club.

'Which brings me to the crux of the matter. We now know of the property developer and how he manipulates both the supply and demand sides of residential development while receiving preferential sites by means of under the table payments for favourable council and political decisions. There seems to be nothing we can do to eliminate this problem. However, what I propose is we gather information on selected individuals, and that includes politicians, organisations and anybody else we suspect of being involved in matters of a nefarious nature, and not necessarily of a criminal nature, and pass that material on to someone in a position to make it awkward for those involved.'

'And have you anyone in mind?' Ron asked.

'Oh, I can think of a specific investigative journalist who harbours similar concerns as I do. I'm sure he would be pleased as Punch to do a bit of character assassination, provided he has indisputable evidence that would stand up in court, once the libel and slander charges start to get thrown around,' Simon replied with a wry grin.

'Well, tell me Simon. I've had a chat with most of the people here this afternoon and can see where they might fit in with your idea. But just what role do you see me playing in this scheme?' Jackie asked as she reached for a handful of peanuts from the table.

'First off, Jackie, we know you're not happy working where you are at the moment. However, you are located in the one position that can provide the details of people who are in contact with the Premier. I think you may obtain far greater job satisfaction if your job description included the identification of particular visitors you might consider being involved in a bit of hanky-panky, if you get my drift. We would leave the selection of possible targets up to your own judgement. And as you are on friendly terms with a bloke in the accounts department, details of any globetrotting by members of parliament that may be seen as a bit questionable might be useful to us and an embarrassment to the person concerned.'

'Sounds good. I'll have a think about it and get back to

you, but it does appeal to my sense of propriety,' Jackie replied before refilling her chardonnay glass.

Turning to Henry, who was in the act of enticing Johnathon L to take the crust from a cucumber sandwich, not a very environmentally correct act, but Johnathon L didn't mind. 'And Henry, as you're in the property development business I've no doubt, you'd like to see a level playing field?'

'In spades and I know just where you're coming from. And, yes, glad to be of any assistance. There's a few of these cowboy development companies I'd like to see get their come-uppance.'

Simon rummaged in the esky and withdrew a tinny of the light amber. 'Okay people, have we any dissenters to the idea if making life difficult for those who deserve having their life made difficult. I don't know about you, Dave, but I think both of us would find character assassination a far more exciting and rewarding prospect than meeting the criminal charged with murder yesterday meeting you on the street today.'

There were no dissenters.

About the Author

John Henderson was born in Singleton in the state of New South Wales, Australia. The family moved to the town of Yass soon afterwards where he spent his younger days before a move to Sydney. John went to Manly Boys' High School, represented the district in cricket and spent a lot of time surfing. He joined the Army in 1968 and toured South Vietnam in 1969-70.

Following his discharge from the Army and a brief stint in the Commonwealth Public Service, John chose to write crime satire. With his dry, cynical sense of humour, The Simon Webster Fiasco series represents an amusing and skeptical view of life and bureaucratic nonsense, as viewed by the author.

John now lives in Canberra with his wife, Jill, and cat, Fergus.

 twitter.com/JohnHenderson07

www.ingramcontent.com/pod-product-compliance
Lightning Source LLC
Chambersburg PA
CBHW070603130626
46556CB00001B/253